Small Town Blues

Aaron Abilene

Published by Syphon Creative, 2023.

SMALL TOWN BLUES

First edition. November 28, 2023.

Copyright © 2023 Aaron Abilene.

ISBN: 979-8223811534

Written by Aaron Abilene.

Also by Aaron Abilene

Slacker
Slacker 2
Slacker: Dead Man Walkin'

Thomas
Quarantine
Contagion

Zombie Bride
Zombie Bride
Zombie Bride 2
Zombie Bride 3

Standalone
The Victims of Pinocchio
A Christmas Nightmare
Pain
Fat Jesus
A Zombie's Revenge
505
The Headhunter
Crash
Tranq
The Island
Dog
The Quiet Man

Small Town Blues

Written by Aaron Abilene

Bucks Prank.

Bubba, Brutus, Cletus and Sally May are seen walking toward Bucks trailer.

Sally May opens the door and walks into the trailer.

Buck is seen lying on the table with a chainsaw stuck in his massive penis and an axe in his neck.

Sally May screams.

Bubba, Brutus and Cletus run into the trailer and see Buck and say "Holy cow".

Sally May: "Who would do this?"

Bubba: "I don't know"

Buck sits up with the axe still stuck in his neck and the chainsaw still stuck in his penis and says "Brains".

Sally May pushes the guys down and runs over them and out the door.

Buck stands up and starts walking toward Bubba, Brutus and Cletus.

Bubba, Brutus and Cletus start crying.

Buck: " You bunch of pussies, it was a joke".

As the adrenaline began to subside, Sally May returned to the trailer with a stern expression on her face. "A joke? You call this a joke?" she spat at Buck, pointing at his still-bloodied groin and neck. "You could have seriously hurt yourself!"

Buck just shrugged and chuckled, and the guys looked at each other with a mix of relief and annoyance.

Sally May shook her head and walked over to the table where Buck lay. "Let me take care of that," she said, grabbing a pair of scissors from a nearby drawer.

Buck winced as she carefully removed the chainsaw from his penis, and then the ax from his neck. She tended to his wounds with practiced ease, muttering under her breath about reckless men and their lack of common sense.

Once Buck was bandaged up and sat up, Sally May turned to Bubba, Brutus, and Cletus. "I think it's time for you boys to go home," she said firmly. "And Buck, I hope you learned your lesson."

The guys shuffled out of the trailer, chastened but relieved that their friend wasn't actually dead. As they walked down the path towards home, they laughed nervously about the close call.

But Sally May stayed behind with Buck, staring him down until he finally looked up at her sheepishly. "I'm sorry," he muttered.

"Damn right you are," she replied. "And don't you forget it."

The three men slowly stand up, still looking horrified. Buck takes the chainsaw out of his penis and the axe out of his neck, wiping away the fake blood and grinning at them.

Buck: "I just had to get you guys back for that time you pretended to drown Bubba in the pond."

Bubba, Brutus and Cletus breathe a sigh of relief and laugh nervously.

Bubba: "You really had us going there, Buck. We thought someone had really done you in."

Sally May walks back into the trailer, her face still white with shock.

Sally May: "Don't ever do that again, Buck. I almost had a heart attack."

Buck looks contrite.

Buck: "Sorry babe, I didn't mean to scare you like that. But you have to admit it was a good prank."

Sally May rolls her eyes but smiles despite herself.

Sally May: "You're lucky I love you, you big lug."

Buck pulls Sally May into his arms and kisses her.

Buck: "I know I am. Now come on, let's go get some beers and forget about this whole thing."

The group leaves the trailer, laughing and joking as they head towards the nearest bar. Despite the scare they just went through, they know that as long as they have each other, they can handle anything that comes their way.

The three guys stood up, relieved that Buck was still alive and well. They nervously chuckled, embarrassed at how easily they fell for Buck's prank. But as they looked closer, they saw that the chainsaw and axe were both fake props, expertly placed to scare Sally May.

Cletus: "You had us good, Buck! That was some next-level stuff."

Brutus: "Yeah man, you really had us thinking we were in a horror movie."

Bubba, still shaking a bit from the scare, added, "I gotta admit, I'm not too fond of these kinds of pranks. My heart can't take it."

Buck laughed heartily and clapped them on their backs. "Come on now boys, don't be such scaredy-cats. We gotta have some excitement around here every once in a while."

As Sally May timidly walked back into the trailer, Buck winked at her. "Sorry about that little scare, darlin'. I couldn't resist."

She playfully rolled her eyes and smiled back at him. "You're lucky I love you."

The group settled down and passed around a bottle of moonshine, swapping stories and laughing about old times. It may have been a close call with the prank, but in the end it brought them all closer together.

But Buck's joke didn't go as planned. The sight of the chainsaw and axe sticking out of his body was so grotesque that it triggered something in him. He began to feel an overwhelming sense of rage building up inside him at the three men who were cowering on the floor.

Bubba, who was always the most confident of the group, slowly got up and approached Buck. "What kind of sick joke is that, Buck?" he asked, his voice shaking.

Buck just chuckled coldly. "I thought you guys could handle a little scare," he said.

But Bubba wasn't having any of it. He raised his fist and punched Buck right in his face. The force of the punch caused Buck to stumble back, and for a moment it seemed like he was about to fall over. But instead he regained his balance and looked at Bubba with cold, dangerous eyes.

"That was a mistake," he growled.

And suddenly, everything changed. Buck's body began to contort and change shape. His skin turned gray and scales started to form all over his body. His eyes glowed with a red light that seemed to penetrate deep into Bubba's soul.

Bubba and the other two men were now completely terrified, realizing they had never seen anything like this before. Sally May had gathered some other people from the campsite who came rushing in and were staring at them in horror.

Then Buck did something that made everyone gasp. He extended his arms and let out an ear-piercing roar that shook the trailer to its very foundation. Everyone who was inside the trailer except Buck himself was scared out of their minds and they ran away from the trailer.

Zombies Arrive.

Zombies are seen walking down the road toward Bucks farm.

Zombies are seen walking all over Bubbas farm.

Zombies are seen on every farm for miles around.

The paved road is filled with zombies.

The mountains surrounding the community are lined with zombies.

Buck's heart pounded in his chest as he stared out at the sea of undead that had descended upon his quiet little farm. He could see them pressing against the fence, moaning and reaching for him with their decaying flesh.

With trembling hands, Buck reached for his shotgun and loaded it with a fresh round. He knew he had to defend himself and his land from these creatures, but he also knew that it was a losing battle. The zombies seemed endless, spreading like a disease across the countryside.

As he took aim at the nearest zombie's head and pulled the trigger, Buck felt a sense of resignation wash over him. He knew that this was no longer his world, that the living had lost to the dead. But he would be damned if he would go down without a fight.

Buck fired shot after shot, taking down zombie after zombie until his gun ran out of ammo. He could hear their footsteps outside, pounding against the door as they tried to break in. Buck backed away slowly, eyes fixed on that door.

Suddenly, there was a loud crash and the door burst open. Buck stumbled backward, falling onto the ground as a group of zombies poured into his house. He tried to fight them off with his bare hands but it was no use. They were too strong.

As they tore into him, Buck gritted his teeth and prepared to meet his end with dignity. He had fought until the bitter end and that was all he could do. The wasteland belonged to the dead now.

Buck gripped the handle of his shotgun tightly as he peered out of the window, watching in horror as the dead walked towards his farm. He had heard the stories from other farmers in the area, but he never thought it would happen to him.

He could see Bubba frantically running around his farm, trying to board up his windows and doors before it was too late. Buck knew that it was only a matter of time until the zombies reached his own property, and he needed to act fast.

He grabbed his backpack, filled it with ammunition and food, and headed out to meet the approaching horde head on. As he stepped outside, the stench of death hit him like a ton of bricks. He had never smelled anything like it before.

Buck took aim at the first zombie that stumbled towards him, and fired. The sound echoed through the quiet countryside, alerting all the nearby undead to his presence. He kept firing until his shotgun clicked empty, then quickly reloaded and continued.

As he fought, Buck realized that this was not just a random outbreak. Someone had intentionally unleashed this plague upon their community, and now it was up to him and others like him to stop it before it spread too far.

He fought for what felt like hours, taking down one zombie after another until finally he stood alone in a sea of corpses. The sun was beginning to rise over the mountains now, casting an eerie glow across the devastated landscape.

Buck dropped to his knees in exhaustion, sweat pouring down his face as he tried to catch his breath. But he knew that this was only the beginning. There were still countless more zombies coming right at him.

Buck sat on his front porch, shotgun in hand, watching as the zombie horde shambled closer to his property. He'd always heard stories of the undead rising to feast on the living, but he had never believed it until now.

He glanced over to his neighbor Bubba's farm and could see the zombies swarming over the fields, devouring the crops and any animals they came across. Buck knew that it was only a matter of time before they made their way to his own farm.

Buck stood up and made his way inside, grabbing a backpack and filling it with supplies. He didn't know how long he would need to survive, but he intended to do whatever it took to outlast the zombie apocalypse.

As he made his way back outside, he checked his shotgun once more before strapping the backpack onto his shoulders. The noise seemed to attract the attention of the zombies, who began to moan and shuffle even closer.

Buck started to back away slowly, eyeing the zombies as they closed in on him. He knew that he couldn't fight all of them off, so he turned and began to run towards the mountains.

He could feel their hands reaching out for him as he ran, but he pushed himself harder than ever before. Finally, after what felt like an eternity, Buck reached a small cave nestled in the mountainside.

He breathed a sigh of relief as he collapsed onto the ground, exhaustion taking hold. Buck had survived this far, but he knew that this was just the beginning of his fight against the undead.

Running.

Zombies enter Bucks farm and move toward Bucks Trailer.

Sally May looks at the zombies and screams and runs back inside the trailer.

Buck: "What's wrong?"

Sally May hits Buck.

Buck: "What the hell was that for?"

Sally May: "You scared me".

Buck hits Sally May knocking her over the coffee table.

Sally May: "What was that for?"

Buck: "You pissed me off."

Sally May: "Sorry, Are all the creeps outside in on your little joke?"

Buck: "No, what creeps?"

Sally May: "The creepy guys outside".

Buck walks toward the door.

Zombies open the door and walk into the trailer.

Buck: "Holy shit".

Zombies look at the group and say "Brains".

Buck: "Okay, bye bye." Runs out the back door followed by Sally May, Bubba, Brutus and Cletus.

A bear is seen behind the trailer.

Sally May : "Bear" Runs away.

Buck looks at the bear and says "Sally May has the right idea." Runs away followed by Bubba, Brutus and Cletus.

The zombies walk out the back door of the trailer.

The bear attacks the zombies.

The group runs into the woods.

A snake crawls up Bubbas pants.

Bubba pulls his pants off and runs away screaming "Snake".

A raccoon falls out of a tree and lands on Bucks head.

Buck throws the raccoon and slams into a tree and falls down.

A tree branch falls and lands on Brutus' head knocking him down.

A skunk sprays Sally May.

Sally May : "Damn it".

A bird craps on Cletus' head.

Sally May laughs and says "Hey shithead."

Cletus: "Shut up Sally Skunk Sauce".

Zombies are seen moving toward the group.

Buck: "Shit , Lets get the horses".

The group runs to get the horses.

As they approach the horses, they notice that one of them is missing. Buck curses under his breath as he realizes that the missing horse was probably taken by the zombies or worse.

Sally May: "What are we going to do? We can't outrun them on foot."

Buck: "We'll have to fight them off until we can find another horse or a vehicle. Everyone grab whatever weapons you can find."

The group starts to scavenge for anything that could be used as a weapon. Sally May picks up a shovel, while Bubba grabs a piece of wood. Cletus finds an old shotgun and Brutus picks up a large rock.

As the zombies get closer, Buck takes charge and leads the group into battle. They swing and hit the zombies with all their might, but more keep coming.

Just when it seems like they're about to be overwhelmed, a caravan of survivors in trucks and armed with guns come to their aid. They mow down the zombies with ease and offer to take Buck and his group with them to their camp.

Buck is hesitant at first, but Sally May urges him to accept the offer. With no other options, they climb into one of the trucks and head towards the survivor's camp.

As they drive away, Buck can't help but think about all the strange events that have happened in the past few hours. It's like every creature in the forest was out to get them.

But for now, he's just grateful that they're still alive and it looks like they might just make it out of this alive after all.

As they reached the stables, Buck quickly prepared the horses for their escape. He could hear the groans of the zombies getting louder as they approached.

Sally May mounted on her horse and turned to see the others struggling to get on theirs. She urged her horse forward, but before she could ride far, she saw a zombie lunging towards her.

Sally May took out her gun and fired at the zombie, its body falling to the ground. She was relieved until she heard a loud hiss behind her. Turning around, she saw a group of snakes slithering towards her.

Buck shouted at Sally May to ride as he took out his own gun and aimed it at the snakes. He shot at them, but they were too many and too quick for him to hit them all.

Bubba had just mounted his horse when he saw one snake sneaking up on him. With a quick reflex, he grabbed it by its tail and flung it away just in time before it sunk its fangs into his leg.

The group managed to fend off the snakes, but they knew that more danger was coming their way. They rode off as fast as they could, leaving behind the zombies and animals that were still fighting each other.

As they rode through the woods, Sally May realized they were lost. They had no idea where they were or where they were headed.

Buck tried to be optimistic as he said, "We just need to keep moving until we find civilization."

The group continued riding until they came across a small town. The streets were deserted except for a few zombies wandering around.

As they reached the horses, they quickly saddled them up and got on. Buck led the way with Sally May close behind him. Bubba, Brutus, and Cletus followed suit.

The sound of the zombies grew closer and closer as they galloped away from the horde. Sally May gripped onto Buck's shirt tightly, trying to ignore the bumpy ride.

Suddenly, Bubba's horse tripped over a rock and stumbled, sending Bubba flying off the saddle. The others reined in their horses to a stop.

Buck: "Come on, we can't just leave him!"

Sally May: "But the zombies -"

Buck: "We'll have to take our chances."

They all dismounted from their horses and ran back toward Bubba, who had hit his head hard on a nearby rock and was unconscious. The sound of groaning zombies grew ever closer.

Cletus: "We gotta pick him up and carry him!"

Brutus: "I'll cover you. Just go!"

The remaining four picked up Bubba and started running again, with Brutus firing his shotgun at any zombie who got too close. Sally May's heart raced with every step she took, but she kept going.

Finally, they reached a small shed near the edge of the woods. Buck kicked open the door and ran inside with the others close behind. They barricaded themselves inside as the zombies pounded on the door, trying to break it down.

Sally May: "What now? How are we going to get out of here?"

As they approached the stables, Buck frantically searched for the keys to the horse stalls. The zombies were closing in quickly, their moans growing louder with each passing second.

Sally May was already on edge due to the bear and the skunk incident, and the thought of being trapped in a stable with the undead made her panic. She began to hyperventilate and shake uncontrollably, making it difficult for Buck to calm her down and find the keys at the same time.

Finally, after what felt like an eternity of searching, Buck found the keys and unlocked the gate. As soon as they were inside, he quickly shut the gate behind them and turned to face Sally May.

"Listen to me," he said sternly. "We need to stay calm and figure out a plan. We can't just hide in here forever."

Bubba, Brutus, and Cletus all nodded in agreement. Sally May took a deep breath and tried to steady herself.

"Okay," she said shakily. "What's the plan?"

Buck thought for a moment before responding. "We need to find a way out of here without being spotted by those things. I suggest we wait until nightfall when it's dark enough for us to sneak past them."

The group nodded in agreement, relieved that Buck had come up with a plan. They settled down with their horses in the stalls, trying to keep themselves occupied as they waited for nightfall.

As darkness fell upon them, Buck signaled for everyone to be quiet. They slowly crept out of the stables one by one, careful not to make any noise that could alert the zombies.

Horsing Around.

They get on their horses and begin to ride away.

Old Man Zombie: "Get back here so I can eat your brains."

Buck: "Shut up or I'll have my horse shit on you."

The zombies start getting closer to the group.

Bubbas horse sees the zombies and the horse jumps on Bubbas back and starts riding him and Bubba says "Get your heavy ass off my back."

The horse says "Ironically enough, that was precisely what I was thinking when you were on my back."

Bubba says "Holy shit." And throws the horse and runs by everyone screaming.

Buck: "What's wrong with Bubba?"

The horse looks at the camera and says "What on earth is his problem?"

Buck: "Lets hide in the barn."

As they enter the barn, Buck bars the door with a broken piece of wood. The group looks around, taking in their surroundings. The barn is filled with hay bales stacked high against the walls. In the center, there's an old tractor and a pile of rusty tools lying next to it.

All of a sudden they hear a scream coming from outside. It's Bubba. They run to the door to see what's happening, but they can't see anything in the darkness.

Old Man Zombie: "I'll check it out."

Buck: "Be careful."

Old Man Zombie steps out into the night, and as soon as his foot touches the ground, a hand grabs him by the ankle and pulls him down. He screams as he's dragged away into the shadows.

Buck slams the door shut and uses the piece of wood to secure it as best he can.

They're trapped.

Samantha: "What are we going to do?"

Buck: "We'll have to wait until dawn."

They sit in silence for hours until finally, rays of sunlight start to peak through the cracks in the barn walls. They slowly make their way out, looking for any sign of danger. As they walk through a field of tall grass, they suddenly hear a low growl coming from behind them. They turn around to see Old Man Zombie standing there, his eyes glowing red.

He lunges at Samantha, but Buck manages to grab a pitchfork and impales him through the chest.

The group continues on, unsure of what other horrors await them in this post-apocalyptic world filled with zombies and danger at every turn.

As they reached the barn, Buck quickly opened the door and ushered everyone in. The stench of hay and manure filled their nostrils as they looked for a place to hide. The sound of moans from outside made them all nervous.

Old Man Zombie: "They won't be able to hide from me for long."

Buck: "We need to find something to board up the door."

Just then, they heard a loud knock on the door. Everyone froze in fear.

Buck: "Who's there?"

Voice: "It's me, Mark. I've been bitten and need your help."

The group hesitated for a moment before Buck finally spoke.

Buck: "Come in, but we need to be careful. We don't know if you'll turn into one of those things."

Mark stumbled in, barely holding himself upright. His skin was pale and his eyes were bloodshot.

Mark: "Please, you have to help me before it's too late."

Buck and Old Man Zombie hesitated, but Bubba stepped forward.

Bubba: "We have to help him. He's still our friend."

They found some wooden planks and began to board up the door. Meanwhile, Mark's condition worsened by the minute.

As they finished boarding up the door, Mark let out a loud scream as he turned into a zombie.

Old Man Zombie: "I told you not to trust him!"

The group backed away as Mark started pounding on the door. They knew they had to find another way out before he broke through.

As they entered the barn, Buck slammed the door shut and leaned against it, panting heavily. The others were staring at him, their faces flushed with fear. Buck looked around and saw that there was no way out of the barn except through the front door, which was now being pounded on by Old Man Zombie and his horde.

Buck: "We need to barricade this door."

The others nodded in agreement, and they quickly got to work. They piled up hay bales, crates, and barrels against the door until there was no way anything could get through. As they worked, Buck's mind raced with thoughts of their situation. He had always known that the zombie apocalypse was a possibility, but he never thought he would actually be facing it.

Suddenly, there was a loud crash as something broke through the roof of the barn. Buck and the others looked up to see a large group of zombies crawling down from the hole.

Buck: "We're screwed."

Just then, there was a bright flash of light, and Buck felt himself being lifted off the ground. He closed his eyes as he felt himself being pulled upwards.

When he opened his eyes again, he found himself in a dark room with no windows. He looked around and saw that the other survivors were there with him.

"What the hell just happened?" Bubba asked.

Buck shook his head. "I don't know. But I think we just got saved."

As they rode towards the barn, Buck saw the bloodthirsty zombies gaining on them and knew they needed a plan. He turned to his trusty sidekick, the horse, and asked for his opinion.

The horse snorted and replied, "We're not getting anywhere with Bubba acting like a fool. We need to stick together and fight these zombies."

Buck nodded in agreement and urged his horse to move faster. As they reached the safety of the barn, Buck began searching for any weapons they could use to fend off the undead attackers.

Suddenly, the door burst open and a group of zombies stumbled inside, their rotting flesh sagging off their bones. Buck readied himself for battle, but was surprised when a voice called out from among the zombies.

"Buck! It's me, your old friend Dave!"

Buck could hardly believe it. Dave had been missing for months and was presumed to be dead. But there he was, standing among a hoard of zombies as if it were nothing.

Dave explained how he had stumbled upon a secret government facility where they were experimenting on the undead and that was why he had been gone so long.

As Buck listened in amazement, he realized that this was their chance to put an end to the zombie apocalypse once and for all. With Dave's insider knowledge and Buck's fearlessness, they would strike a blow against the undead that would send shockwaves through the world.

Together, they hatched a plan to infiltrate the facility and stop the experiments before it was too late. The fate of humanity rested on their shoulders, but Buck knew that with Dave by his side they would survive.

Hiding in the barn.

The group enters the barn.

Cletus: "Okay, What's next?"

Buck: "I don't know, I've never been hunted by talking dead people before."

Bubba : "I saw this movie before and they seemed to kill them by shooting them in the head or destroying the brain."

Sally May: " How often does anything you see in a movie actually work in real life?"

Buck: "That's like saying you saw Brad Pitt pick up a girl in a movie but when you try that same method , you come home with a black eye 3 missing teeth and a high heel shoe in your ass. That's when it hits you that , that type of thing doesn't work unless it's a movie and another thing that comes to mind is, you should never follow an actress home to try and ask her out because they have mean guard dogs."

Brutus: " Well, we should at least get some guns to protect ourselves."

The group exits the barn.

As they stepped out of the barn, the moon was high up in the sky. The howling of wolves echoed throughout the forest. Cletus looked around nervously. He knew something was coming.

Suddenly, a loud growl filled the air. Everyone froze in fear as they saw a group of zombies slowly approaching them. Buck pulled out his gun and aimed it at them.

"Wait," Sally May said, "we need to find a way to get rid of them for good."

Bubba nodded in agreement and added, "Yeah, shooting them in the head only buys us time. We need something more permanent."

Brutus looked around frantically, searching for any kind of weapon he could use against the zombies. His eyes locked onto a chainsaw lying on the ground nearby.

"I've got an idea," he said as he picked up the chainsaw. "Follow me!"

The group followed Brutus as he charged towards the zombies with his chainsaw roaring loudly. The zombies were caught off guard by the sudden attack and started to fall to pieces under the sharp blade.

The group fought bravely against the undead horde with Buck's gun and Brutus' chainsaw taking out every zombie that came their way.

After what seemed like hours, the last zombie fell to the ground lifeless. The group stood there panting, covered in blood and sweat.

Cletus let out a deep sigh of relief as he looked at his friends. "I have a feeling this is just the beginning," he said, "we need to be ready for anything."

As they stepped outside, a chilling breeze sent shivers down their spines. The moon was high up in the sky, casting eerie shadows on the ground. They made their way towards the shed where they kept their weapons.

Cletus unlocked the door and they stepped inside. The scent of gunpowder filled the air as they searched for suitable firearms.

Sally May grabbed a shotgun and inspected it carefully. Buck opted for a revolver while Bubba settled for a hunting rifle. Brutus, on the other hand, picked up an axe from the corner of the shed.

As they were about to leave, they heard a rustling sound coming from outside.

Brutus signaled everyone to stay quiet and cautiously opened the door. Suddenly, a group of zombies jumped out from behind the bushes and charged at them.

Cletus fired his shotgun, taking down two of them while Sally May aimed her weapon at another one's head and pulled the trigger.

Buck fired his revolver but missed his target, hitting a nearby tree instead. Bubba, however, had better luck with his rifle and managed to take out one of the zombies from a distance.

Just when they thought they had overcome the undead assailants, several more appeared from behind the trees and surrounded them.

Brutus swung his axe with all his might, fending off the creatures that came too close while the others continued to shoot at them.

Finally, after what seemed like an eternity, all of the zombies were dead. The group gathered their weapons and headed back towards the barn, knowing that this was only the beginning of their battle against the undead.

As they stepped out of the barn, Brutus led the way towards a nearby shed. Once they reached it, he picked up a rusty axe from the ground. Buck rolled his eyes.

"An axe is not going to do much against a horde of flesh-eating zombies," he said.

Brutus shrugged. "It's better than nothing."

Sally May spotted a shotgun tucked away in the corner and grabbed it. "This will be more useful," she said, checking to see if it was loaded.

Bubba found a couple of pistols hanging on a pegboard and handed one to Cletus. "Keep this close," he instructed.

The group began to walk towards the main house when they heard a sound behind them. They turned around to find two zombies standing at the entrance of the barn, their eyes fixed on the group.

Everyone reached for their weapons as the zombies started to shuffle closer. Sally May took aim and fired her shotgun, blowing off one of the zombie's heads. Cletus fired his pistol, but missed and hit a nearby tree. Buck swung his axe but only managed to chop off a few fingers before he was tackled to the ground by the other zombie.

Brutus rushed forward with his axe and landed a blow on the zombie's head, killing it instantly. Buck stood up, brushing dirt off his shirt.

"Thanks, man," he said to Brutus.

"No problem," Brutus replied, looking around nervously.

Suddenly, they heard more groaning sounds coming from behind them. The group turned around to see a whole horde of zombies heading their way.

"We need to find somewhere better to hide."

As they stepped out of the barn, they heard a faint growling noise coming from the bushes. Buck quickly grabbed his shotgun and aimed it at the bush. Suddenly, a huge zombie dog jumps out and charges at the group.

Sally May screams, "Shoot it! Shoot it!"

But Buck hesitates as he looks into the eyes of the undead animal. He sees something familiar in its eyes, a connection to his own beloved pet dog that he had to leave behind when the apocalypse began.

Cletus yells, "Buck, for Christ's sake! Pull the trigger!"

With tears streaming down his face, Buck finally pulls the trigger, blasting the creature's head off. As the group catches their breath, they realize they have a tough road ahead of them.

"We need to find more guns and ammo," Brutus said. "And fast."

They set off down the dirt road, with their shadows growing longer as the sun sank low in the sky. The smell of death hung heavy in the air, but they had to keep moving forward if they wanted to survive.

Running thru the woods.

The group begins running thru the woods.

A zombie walks out from behind a tree.

Buck grabs the zombie and throws it to Bubba and continues running.

Bubba throws the zombie to Cletus and continues running.

Cletus throws the zombie to Brutus and continues running.

Brutus throws the zombie to Sally May and continues running.

Sally May throws the zombie to another zombie and continues running.

The group runs out of the woods and run towards the building where they keep their guns.

As they approached the building, Buck led the charge with his shotgun. The others followed close behind, adrenaline pumping through their veins.

They burst through the doors, guns at the ready, but were met with an unexpected sight - the room was empty. Their weapons were gone.

In a panic, they started to search for any clues as to who could have taken their guns. They scoured every inch of the room until Sally May spotted a piece of paper on the ground.

With shaking hands, she picked it up and read the message aloud: "I have your weapons. If you want them back, come find me."

The group glanced around at one another in fear. Who could have taken their guns and why?

Buck stepped forward, determined to get answers. "We'll split up and search for this person," he declared. "But be on high alert - we don't know what we're dealing with."

The group nodded in agreement and quickly separated, each taking a different route in search of their missing weapons.

As Sally May ran through the dark alleyways, she stumbled upon a figure lurking in the shadows. Her heart racing with terror, she raised her gun and demanded to know where their weapons were.

The figure stepped forward, revealing himself to be a tall, muscular man with piercing blue eyes. In his hand was a single bullet - the only thing left of their arsenal.

He grinned devilishly. "You shouldn't have underestimated me," he taunted. "Now suffer the consequences."

Sally May knew she was in deep trouble. She was outnumbered and outgunned with no backup in sight. But she refused to give up

As they approach the building, they can hear the sound of moaning zombies inside. Buck motions for everyone to stay back as he sneaks up to the door. Carefully peeking inside, he sees a group of zombies huddled around their stash of guns and ammo.

Buck signals to the others to follow his lead and they all move in quickly and quietly. Sally May pulls out her trusty machete, Brutus grabs a nearby pipe, Cletus finds a crowbar, Bubba picks up a wooden plank, and Buck grabs a hunting knife from his belt.

The group attacks the zombies with precision, taking them down one by one with brutal efficiency. They make quick work of the undead horde and soon have all their guns and ammo back in their possession.

As they exit the building, they can see more zombies approaching in the distance. But this time, they're prepared. Buck hands out weapons to everyone and gives orders on how to best take down the oncoming threat.

And so they stand ready for whatever comes next, unified in their fight against the zombie apocalypse.

As they approach the building, Buck slams his hand against the door, pushing it open. The hinges creak loudly, echoing through the empty street.

"Grab your weapons!" Buck shouts, and the group rushes inside.

The room is dimly lit, illuminated only by the light filtering in through boarded up windows. There are rows of weapons lining the walls: handguns, shotguns, assault rifles - enough to arm an army.

Bubba strides to a rack of shotguns and pulls one down, checking the chamber. Cletus grabs a pistol, checking its magazine before tucking it into his waistband. Brutus reaches for an M4 but hesitates, staring blankly at the wall.

Sally May takes in a deep breath and walks over to him. "What's wrong?" she asks.

"I... I can't do this," he replies. "I don't know if I can kill people like they're nothing."

Sally May puts a hand on his shoulder. "They're not people anymore," she says firmly. "They're monsters that want to rip us apart. You have to protect yourself and all of us."

Brutus nods slowly, grasping the M4 and checking its magazine. The others finish arming themselves and head towards the exit.

"Let's go," Buck says, pushing past them.

Once outside, they set off down the street towards safety. But suddenly gunshots ring out from behind them, followed by a scream.

They whirl around to see Sally May on the ground, blood seeping from a wound in her side. A small group of zombies is closing in on her.

As they approach the building, they notice something odd. The once impenetrable metal door seems to have been partially ripped open. Buck approaches cautiously, peering inside.

"Guys, you won't believe it," Buck whispers urgently, "There's a group of survivors in there!"

The rest of the group hurry over to see for themselves. They can barely contain their excitement as they spot the other survivors huddled in a corner of the room, their eyes filled with fear.

Bubba takes charge, signaling to the others that they should circle around and trap the zombies between them. The group slowly moves into position as Sally May hands out guns to all the survivors.

Suddenly, one of the zombies charges towards Brutus. Without missing a beat, he takes aim and fires his shotgun, taking the zombie out with ease.

As they continue to fight off the endless horde of zombies, Sally May finds herself standing back-to-back with one of the other survivors. Her heart is pounding in her chest as she realizes that she's surrounded.

Just when it seems like all hope is lost, Buck spots a crack in one of the walls. He signals for everyone to follow him as they make a break for it.

Once they're on the other side, they take a moment to catch their breath and survey their surroundings. It seems like they've stumbled upon a small town that has managed to survive despite everything that has happened.

With renewed hope, the group continues on their journey, knowing that no matter what lies ahead, they'll face it together.

Lock & Load.

The group enters the gun shed, its walls are lined with guns, the floor is full of guns and ammo. There are glass display cases full of pistols.

Buck fills a duffle bag with guns and ammo.

Bubba fills a duffle bag with guns and ammo.

Cletus fills a duffle bag with guns and ammo.

Brutus fills a duffle bag with guns and ammo.

Sally May fills a duffle bag with guns and ammo and gives it to Buck.

Buck: " I've got an idea, keep filling bags with weapons and ammo. I'll be right back."

The group continues filling the duffle bags with weapons and ammo.

Buck walks out of the gun shed and walks around back and uncovers the weapons truck already fully loaded with rpgs and all kinds of explosives and drives it to the front of the gun shed and goes back in the gun shed and says "Lets load it up."

Sally May: "What?"

Buck: "Load all the bags in the truck."

Sally May: "What truck?"

Buck: "The truck outside."

The group loads all the bags in the truck and drive away.

As they drove into the night, the adrenaline from their latest heist still pumping through their veins, Buck couldn't help but feel a familiar thrill. It was the feeling of power, of being in control. He loved it.

The group eventually made it to their hideout, a dingy old motel on the outskirts of town. They quickly unloaded the weapons and ammo, spreading them out on the bed for inspection.

Bubba whistled at the sight. "We hit the jackpot this time, boys and girls."

Cletus nodded in agreement as he looked over the arsenal. "Yeah man, we're gonna be unstoppable with all this firepower."

But Sally May couldn't shake the uneasy feeling that had settled in her stomach. Sure, they had just pulled off a major score, but at what cost? The more she thought about it, the more she realized that this life of crime was starting to wear on her.

As Buck began divvying up the weapons and assigning tasks for their next job, Sally May quietly slipped out of the room. She needed some fresh air.

As she walked down the empty motel hallway, she noticed a door slightly ajar. Curiosity getting the best of her, she pushed it open to reveal a dimly lit room.

At first glance, it appeared to be a small office with a desk and filing cabinets lining the walls. But as Sally May approached the desk, something caught her eye - a small framed picture.

It was of a young girl with curly brown hair and bright green eyes. Sally May's heart sank as she recognized herself.

Suddenly, memories of her past flooded back - before she ever knew any of these guys.

As they drove away, the adrenaline ran high in Buck's veins. He knew that they needed to act fast if they wanted to come out of this alive. The sun was setting and the sky was painted red, orange and gold, creating a beautiful but eerie atmosphere. The silence inside the truck was deafening as everyone contemplated what was about to come.

Buck finally broke the silence and spoke up, "Listen up y'all. We've got a job to do and it ain't gonna be easy. But we gotta do it anyway for our families and our land."

Everyone nodded in agreement as they pulled up to the entrance of the enemy's hideout. Buck parked the truck a few feet away from their location and turned off the engine. They all grabbed their bags of weapons, loaded their guns and started walking towards the entrance.

The closer they got, the louder their footsteps echoed against the rocks and trees surrounding them. After what felt like hours, they finally made it to the entrance of the enemy's hideout. Buck signaled everyone to ready their weapons and take cover as he slowly opened the door.

As soon as he opened it, gunshots rang out from inside, bullets whizzing past them in every direction. They all huddled close together for protection as Buck called out to them, "We gotta push through y'all! Keep firing!"

They all obeyed his command and began firing back while moving forward through the enemy's hideout. The noise was deafening with bullets flying everywhere, hitting walls and ricocheting off rocks.

But Buck knew that he couldn't give up now. He had a mission to accomplish and nothing would stop until it was over.

As the truck bounces along the dirt road, Sally May can't help but feel a sense of unease. She'd always known the group was involved in some shady dealings, but this was different. This was dangerous.

Buck grins over at her, his eyes gleaming in the moonlight. "You nervous, darlin'?" he asks with a chuckle.

She swallows hard, trying to push down her fear. "Should we really be doing this?" she asks, gesturing towards the bags of weapons and explosives piled high in the back of the truck.

Buck just laughs. "Relax, Sally May. We're gonna make a killing with all these goodies. The client is gonna be very happy."

Sally May nods, not quite convinced. She leans back against the seat and watches as they approach a rundown warehouse on the outskirts of town.

Brutus pulls the truck up to the loading dock and they all jump out, grabbing bags of weapons and explosives as they go.

Once inside, they find themselves in a dimly lit room filled with shady looking characters. One of them steps forward, eyeing Buck's crew suspiciously.

"You got what we asked for?" he growls.

Buck steps forward confidently, slapping a bag full of guns onto the table. "We got everything you need right here," he says with a grin.

The man opens up the bag and inspects the goods inside before nodding approvingly. "Looks good," he says, handing over a briefcase full of cash.

As they count out their earnings, Sally May can't help but feel relieved that everything is going their way.

The sound of the engine roars as they drive down the empty road, heading towards their destination. Sally May looks out the window, thinking about their plan and what they're about to do. She had been with the group for a while and knew what they were capable of, but this time felt different. She had a sense of unease in her stomach that she couldn't quite shake.

As they arrive at their target location, Buck parks the truck and turns to address the group.

"Alright everyone, here's the plan," Buck says with a determined look in his eyes. "We're going to storm the building and take out anyone inside. We have the element of surprise and with all these weapons, we can't lose."

The group nods in agreement, all too eager to use their new gear.

Sally May takes a deep breath and looks over at Brutus. His eyes meet hers and she sees something in them that she hasn't seen before - fear. It surprises her because Brutus always seemed fearless, like he was invincible.

Buck hands out instructions and puts his plan into action. They move quickly and quietly, preparing for what's ahead. As they approach the building, they split into smaller groups to cover more ground.

Sally May's group enters through a side door, guns at the ready. The adrenaline pumps through her veins as she moves through the building, taking out anyone that gets in their way. She can hear gunshots from other parts of the building and knows that Buck's group is doing their job too.

As they make their way to the main floor, Sally May sees a figure in the distance.

Sheriff.

Cletus: "You think we should tell the sheriff?"

Buck: "He'll find out sooner or later."

The group is seen driving down the 2 lane road headed to town.

The sheriff is seen driving the opposite direction down the road.

Bubba: " There goes the sheriff."

Sally May: "Someone better tell him not to go that way."

Everyone yells: "Don't go that way, sheriff."

Sheriff: "Crazy hillbillies."

Zombies surround the sheriff.

Sheriff: "What in Sam hell?"

Buck shoots the sheriffs car with an rpg and says "We can't have him becoming a zombie."

The explosion echoed throughout the forest as Buck's laughter filled the air. The group watched with grim satisfaction as the sheriff's car went up in flames, enveloping the zombies in a fiery embrace. Cletus shook his head, marveling at how quickly things had spiraled out of control.

"I can't believe this is happening," he said, his voice shaking. "We were just supposed to go fishing."

Sally May placed a comforting hand on Cletus's shoulder. "I know, honey. But we can't change what's already happened. All we can do now is keep moving forward."

Bubba snorted. "Forward? To where? We don't have a plan."

"We'll figure it out," Sally May said firmly.

But as they drove deeper into the forest, the group's fears grew stronger. They had no idea what was waiting for them in town, or if there was even a town left to go to. The world had gone to hell and they were just trying to survive.

As night fell and the moon cast an eerie glow over the landscape, Cletus suddenly hit the brakes. The others jolted awake, startled by the sudden stop.

"What's going on?" Buck asked groggily.

Cletus pointed toward a clearing up ahead. "Look."

A small group of survivors had gathered around a campfire, their faces illuminated by the flickering flames. Sally May breathed a sigh of relief and pulled over.

"Thank God," she whispered.

Bubba climbed out of the car and walked toward the campfire. The survivors looked up as he approached, their eyes filled with suspicion.

The explosion from the RPG echoed through the countryside. Cletus and Bubba whooped as they high-fived each other, while Sally May and the others looked on in horror. Buck, on the other hand, seemed unaffected by his actions. He merely lit a cigar and took a deep drag as he watched the wreckage burn.

"Well, that takes care of that," Buck said, blowing out a thick plume of smoke.

"Are you crazy?" Sally May screeched. "You just killed the sheriff!"

"He was already dead to begin with," Buck said with a shrug. "Just like all those things out there."

"But he was still human!" Sally May protested.

Buck rolled his eyes. "He was going to turn eventually. Better to take care of it now than let him suffer like the rest of them."

Cletus nodded in agreement. "Buck's right. We did what we had to do."

Sally May shook her head in disbelief. She couldn't believe how callous these people had become since the zombie outbreak began. It was like they had lost all sense of humanity.

As they continued down the road, Sally May couldn't shake the image of the sheriff's burning car from her mind. She knew they were all in danger, but she couldn't help thinking that maybe they had gone too far this time.

Cletus looked over at Buck and rolled his eyes. He knew that Buck had a love for explosives, but he was concerned about the consequences that would follow. "Buck, what the hell? You could have killed the sheriff!" Cletus shouted.

Buck shrugged and grinned. "Better safe than sorry," he said, as he watched the sheriff's car explode into flames. The group watched as the zombies approached the burning car, only to be stopped by an invisible barrier.

Sally May gasped. "What is that?" she asked.

Buck looked at her smugly. "My latest invention," he said. "A zombie force field."

Cletus shook his head in disbelief. "You're insane," he muttered.

But their attention was quickly diverted back to the road when they saw a group of survivors coming towards them. The survivors were driving old trucks, and they looked like they had been through hell and back. They were covered in dirt and blood, and their eyes were wide with terror.

Cletus motioned for the group to stop, and they got out of their cars to meet the survivors. The survivors looked around nervously, and one of them spoke up. "We need your help," she said. "Our camp was overrun by zombies, and we've been on the run ever since."

Cletus looked at his group and nodded. "We'll help you," he said. "But we need to stick together if we're going to survive."

As the sheriff's car explodes into a fiery wreck, the group of hillbillies cheers.

"Yeehaw! That'll keep 'em safe from the zombie hordes!" Cletus exclaimed.

But Sally May wasn't so sure. "I don't know about this, y'all. That was the lawman. What if someone comes looking for him?"

Bubba shrugged. "It don't matter none. Ain't nobody comin' out here anyways."

But just then, a loud rumbling could be heard in the distance.

"What in tarnation is that?" Buck asked.

Suddenly, a convoy of military vehicles appeared on the horizon, all heading straight for them.

The group knew they were in trouble. They had no idea what the military would do to them for killing the sheriff and destroying his car.

But they had no time to run or hide. The convoy was already upon them.

As the vehicles screeched to a halt, heavily armed soldiers jumped out and surrounded the hillbillies.

"Get on your knees!" one of the soldiers shouted.

Cletus, Buck, Bubba, and Sally May complied, their hearts pounding with fear.

"We have reason to believe you were responsible for the death of Sheriff Jenkins," another soldier said, pointing his gun at them.

The hillbillies tried to protest their innocence, but it was no use. The soldiers weren't listening.

And so, in a flash of gunfire and chaos, Cletus, Buck, Bubba, and Sally May met their end at the hands of the military.

All because they had taken matters into their own hands and killed.

Into the city.

The group continues down the 2 lane road into the city.

Bubba: "Where to?"

Buck: "Lets go to the cemetery."

Bubba: "Why would we want to do a stupid thing like that?"

Buck: "Because if we don't go to the cemetery the dead will rise and turn more people into zombies giving us less of a chance to survive."

Bubba: "You've got a point."

The group goes to the cemetery.

As they walked through the cemetery, the air was thick with the stench of rotting corpses. Buck led the way, his eyes scanning for any signs of movement among the headstones. Bubba followed close behind, his grip tight on his machete.

Suddenly, Buck froze in his tracks. Bubba bumped into him, almost knocking him over.

"What the hell, man?" Bubba muttered.

Buck didn't respond. His eyes were glued to a freshly-dug grave in front of them. Bubba followed his gaze and saw something that made his blood run cold.

There was a hand sticking out of the ground.

Buck approached cautiously, gripping his shotgun tightly. As he got closer, he saw that there were several hands emerging from the dirt.

"They're coming up," Buck said grimly.

Bubba's heart was pounding as they backed away slowly. Suddenly, a corpse burst forth from the ground with a furious moan. Buck fired off a shot, blasting a hole through its head.

But it was too late. More corpses were crawling up from their graves, their decayed bodies writhing with hunger and desire for flesh.

Bubba swung his machete wildly as Buck opened fire with his shotgun. But they were outnumbered and outmatched. The zombies closed in, tearing at their flesh with ravenous hunger.

In their final moments, they realized that going to the cemetery had been a terrible mistake. They should have kept moving, kept searching for a safe haven in this world gone mad with death and destruction. But now it was too late. The zombies had won.

As they entered the cemetery, the group could feel the weight of death and decay in the air. The ground was wet and muddy, with gravestones crooked and dilapidated. Buck led them through the overgrown weeds to a small mausoleum at the far end of the graveyard. With a loud creak, Buck pushed open the heavy stone door, revealing a set of dusty stairs leading down to a dark and musty room.

"This is it," Buck said as he descended the stairs. "This is where we'll find what we need."

Bubba and the others followed Buck closely, their hearts racing with anticipation and fear. The room was pitch black, but Buck lit a torch and held it high, illuminating the walls covered in strange symbols and markings.

"Watch your step," Buck warned as they made their way deeper into the room. "There are traps everywhere."

Suddenly, they heard a faint moaning coming from the darkness ahead. Bubba's heart raced as they cautiously approached a large stone pedestal in the center of the room.

"Stop!" Buck shouted as they got closer. "It's a zombie!"

Sure enough, a figure rose from behind the pedestal - a decaying corpse with hollow eyes and rotting flesh.

Without hesitation, Bubba pulled out his machete and charged at the zombie. The others followed suit, fighting off wave after wave of undead until they reached their goal - an ancient book bound in leather and adorned with gold symbols.

Buck opened the book and began to read aloud from its pages. The words were ancient and powerful, calling forth forces beyond human comprehension.

As they entered the cemetery gate, the group was met by a cold and eerie fog. The gravestones were old and weathered, some knocked over and broken. Buck led them through the maze of tombstones until they reached an old crypt at the far end.

"We have to go inside," Buck said with a serious tone.

Bubba hesitated, "Are you sure about this?"

But Buck was already pushing the heavy stone door open, revealing a dark and musty room. They cautiously stepped inside, the sound of their footsteps echoing off the walls.

As their eyes adjusted to the darkness, they saw that the room was filled with coffins. And one of them was slightly open.

Suddenly, a hand reached out from the coffin and grabbed Buck by the ankle. He screamed in horror as he realized what was happening - they were surrounded by zombies.

The group fought back with all their might, using whatever weapons they had brought along. Bubba had a shotgun, while Billy had a machete and Jenny had a baseball bat.

As they battled, they noticed that one of the zombies was different from all the others. It was dressed in tattered clothes with long black hair flowing down its back. Its eyes glowed red with an otherworldly fire.

Buck recognized it immediately, "We have to kill her! She's controlling all these zombies!"

With newfound determination, they hacked away at the horde until they were finally able to strike down the female zombie. As she fell to the ground, her eyes lost their glow and all of the other zombies crumbled into dust.

Breathless but victorious, the group stumbled out of the cemetery.

As they enter the cemetery, the scent of death and decay fills their nostrils. Buck leads the group to a small chapel in the middle of the grounds. The door creaks as he pushes it open, revealing a spiral staircase leading into darkness.

Without hesitation, Buck descends the stairs followed by Bubba and the others. The air grows colder as they go deeper and deeper underground until they reach a large room illuminated by several candles.

In the center of the room stands a dark figure draped in a cloak, their face hidden in shadows.

Buck approaches the figure and bows his head in respect. "Master," he says, "we have come to offer our service."

The figure nods and speaks in a voice that sends shivers down their spines. "Good. You will carry out a task for me."

Bubba looks around nervously as Buck steps forward to receive the instructions. Suddenly, the figure lunges forward and grabs Buck by the throat.

Bubba and the others try to intervene, but they are no match for the figure's strength. As Buck struggles for air, the figure whispers in his ear.

"When you rise again, you will serve me. You will be my loyal slave for eternity."

With those words, Buck falls to the ground lifeless, his eyes staring blankly ahead.

Bubba and the others stand frozen in horror as they realize they have just made a deal with death itself.

Cemetery.

The group drives around the cemetery waiting for bodies to rise from the grave.

An old man is seen walking thru the cemetery with a shovel in his hand.

Zombies are seen rising from the grave throughout the cemetery.

The group open fire on the zombies.

The old man hits zombies over the head with the shovel.

More zombies are seen rising from the grave.

A zombie attacks the old man and bites a chunk out of his forehead.

The group shoots the old man and the remaining zombies.

Buck: "Lets go to the police department."

The group leave the cemetery and go to the police department.

As they sped away from the cemetery, the group couldn't help but feel paranoid. What if the old man was infected? What if they were all infected now? The thought made them shudder.

They arrived at the police department a few minutes later. The building was dark and empty, but they could hear faint moaning sounds coming from inside.

"Looks like we're not alone," Buck said, as he took out his gun.

The group cautiously made their way inside, guns drawn. They saw a few zombies stumbling around in the darkness, and quickly took them down. As they moved further into the building, they found a room filled with supplies.

"We hit the jackpot," one of them exclaimed, as he started filling his backpack with canned food and water bottles.

Suddenly, they heard a loud banging on the door. They turned around and saw a group of zombies trying to break in.

"We need to barricade this place!" Buck shouted.

The group quickly worked together to reinforce the door and windows with anything they could find. But it wasn't enough. The zombies broke through and chaos ensued.

As they fought for their lives, one by one, members of the group fell. It seemed that all hope was lost. But then, just when they thought it was over, a bright light shone outside the window.

"Hey!" a voice called out. "Are you guys okay?"

The group turned around to see a military vehicle parked outside. They had been saved!

As they climbed aboard, exhausted but relieved, Buck couldn't believe what had just happened. It felt like a nightmare that he couldn't wake up from.

As they speed away from the cemetery, Buck taps his fingers nervously against the steering wheel. He couldn't believe what he just witnessed - the dead rising from their graves and attacking the living. As they approach the police department, he can feel his heart racing.

When they arrive, they find that chaos has already taken over. The streets are littered with corpses, some of them still moving, others lying still. The scent of rot fills the air.

Buck and the group rush into the station, looking for any sign of law enforcement. But all they find are empty desks and abandoned cells. It's as if everyone had fled the scene.

Suddenly, a loud banging is heard from one of the cells. Buck cautiously approaches the source of the noise and peers through the small window. What he sees makes him recoil in terror - a group of zombies bashing their heads against the cell door.

Buck turns to the group, his voice shaking. "We need to get out of here. Now." But it's too late – one of the zombies has broken through and is making its way towards them.

The group opens fire, but it's too late for Buck - he's already been bitten. As he feels his body start to change, he makes a decision.

"Leave me," he says, holding back tears. "Don't let me become one of them."

The group hesitates for a moment before finally nodding in agreement. They leave Buck behind as they make their way out into the world overrun by zombies.

But as they drive away, they hear a faint voice calling out from behind them - a now-zombified Buck,

The car sped down the empty road, the group in shock at what they had just witnessed. The old man, who had appeared to be a cemetery caretaker, now lay lifeless in the center of the graveyard. His shovel lay beside him, bloodied and bent from the force of his attacks on the undead. The group knew they had no choice but to head to the police department and report what they had seen.

As they pulled up to the station, they could see that something was wrong. The building was dark, and there were no police cars parked outside. Buck turned off the car and approached the door cautiously. He tried the handle, but it was locked tight.

As Buck attempted to force open the door, a sound caught everyone's attention. It was coming from one of the nearby alleys. The group turned their heads just in time to see a group of zombies making their way towards them.

Without hesitating, they ran back to the car and drove as fast as they could down the empty streets. It wasn't long before they found themselves surrounded by hordes of undead creatures.

In a moment of desperation, Buck turned into an abandoned warehouse on the outskirts of town. The group piled out of the car and barricaded themselves inside, hoping that they had found a safe haven.

But as night fell, they realized that they were far from safe. The zombies outside were relentless, constantly beating against the walls and attempting to break through their barricades.

As dawn finally broke and the zombies outside began to disperse, the group knew that they couldn't stay in their makeshift fortress forever. They had to find a way out before it was too late.

As they drove away from the cemetery, Buck's mind was racing. He knew they needed to report what had happened, but he couldn't help thinking about the old man. Had he been infected? Was he going to turn into a zombie himself?

They arrived at the police department and quickly made their way inside. Buck explained to the officer at the front desk what had happened at the cemetery, leaving out the part about shooting the old man.

The officer stared at Buck in disbelief, but eventually called for backup. Within minutes, a squad car arrived and two officers led Buck and his group to a back room for questioning.

It wasn't until hours later that they were allowed to leave. Buck's mind was still reeling from everything that had happened.

As they made their way back to their car, they were met by a strange figure in the shadows. It was the old man, his eyes now glowing bright red.

Buck instinctively reached for his gun, but before he could even aim it, the old man lunged at him with surprising speed.

The group fought back as best they could, but it was clear that this was not a normal zombie. This was something much more powerful.

In the end, it was Sarah who managed to take down the old man. She grabbed his shovel and swung with all her might, decapitating him in one swift blow.

As they gathered their wits and prepared to leave once again, Buck couldn't help but feel a sense of unease. This was only the beginning of what was sure to be a long and terrifying battle against the undead.

Police Department.

The group enters the police department.

Desk Officer: "Can I help you?"

Buck: "Yeah, I know this is going to sound strange but there are dead people eating the living and I think you should send the big guns to patrol the city."

Desk Officer: " Yeah sure and maybe Angelina Jolie will be naked in my bed when I get home tonight."

A zombie walks into the room with the desk officer.

Buck shoots the zombie.

Desk Officer: "Holy crap, I think I just shit my pants."

Buck: "Yeah I know I smell it. Look , call the military or something the city needs to be evacuated asap. There are more zombies coming this way."

Desk Officer: "Okay."

Buck: " We're going to see if they made it to the hospital and if they did there could be hundreds if not thousands of them."

Desk Officer: "Okay."

The group leaves the police department heading for the hospital.

The desk officer calls the military, swat team and special forces.

Military forces are seen moving into the city.

Swat and all other law enforcement are seen patrolling the city.

As the group gets closer to the hospital, they begin to hear the sounds of screams and moans. Buck turns to the others.

"We need to be careful," he whispers. "There's no telling how many of them are inside."

They approach the entrance cautiously, guns at the ready. As they push through the doors, they're met with a scene straight out of a horror movie.

Zombies are everywhere, feasting on the living. Blood and guts are splattered across the walls and floors. The stench is overwhelming.

The group begins to fight their way through the hordes of undead. Buck has never seen anything like this before - it's like the world has gone mad.

As they make their way deeper into the hospital, they come across a group of survivors who've managed to barricade themselves in a room.

"Thank god," one of them cries as Buck and his team burst in. "We were starting to think we were the only ones left."

Buck assesses the situation quickly. There's no way they can stay here - it's only a matter of time before the zombies break through their defenses.

"We need to move," he says. "We're going to get you out of here."

They manage to make it out of the hospital, but not without losing a few of their own along the way. As they regroup outside, Buck looks around at what's become of his city.

He knows it's not over yet - there are still more zombies out there, waiting to attack. But for now, he's just grateful that he and his team have made it out alive.

As the group makes their way towards the hospital, they're met with the sight of absolute chaos. The once busy streets are littered with abandoned cars and scattered belongings. Buildings on either side of the road crumble, and screams echo in the distance. Buck leads the way, his gun at the ready as they carefully tread through the debris.

They can hear the groans of the undead growing louder with every step they take. Soon, they hear a frantic voice over their radio. It's Sarah - she's in trouble.

Buck picks up his pace, sprinting towards the hospital as fast as he can. The rest of the group follows closely behind him. As they approach, they see Sarah backed up against a wall, surrounded by a hoard of flesh-eating monsters.

Without hesitation, Buck shoots down any zombie that crosses his path, while Jack pulls Sarah to safety. The group rallies together, fighting off wave after wave of the undead as they make their way deeper into the hospital.

It's clear that there's no hope for anyone who's been bitten by one of these things. They've all turned into zombies themselves, and it's only a matter of time before they start attacking everyone around them.

After what seems like hours of fighting through hordes of zombies, the group finally makes it to the roof of the hospital. There, they find a helicopter waiting to take them away to safety.

As they take off into the sky and watch as the city below fades into nothingness, Buck can't help but think about what caused this apocalypse. How did it happen? Could it have been prevented?

As the group makes their way towards the hospital, they notice that the streets are eerily empty. The only sounds they can hear are their own footsteps and the occasional growls of the undead creatures. Buck leads the way, with his shotgun at the ready, while the others follow closely behind him.

As they turn a corner, they come face to face with a group of zombies. Without hesitation, Buck raises his shotgun and takes them down one by one, with the others helping to finish off any stragglers. They continue on their way, encountering more zombies along the path.

Finally, they arrive at the hospital and what they see is nothing short of a nightmare. The place is overrun with zombies and there are bloody handprints on every surface. They can hear moaning and groaning coming from every room.

Buck turns to his group and says, "We have to be quick and quiet. Stick together and stay alert." They nod in agreement, knowing that they must move swiftly if they want to survive.

They make their way through the hospital, killing any zombies that get in their way. As they turn a corner, a zombie lunges at Buck and knocks him to the ground. The others quickly come to his rescue, but as they're fighting off the creature, Buck notices something strange about it. Its skin is crawling with maggots and its eyes look different somehow.

He manages to kill it with one final shot from his shotgun before turning to the others and saying, "We need to get out of here right now. These aren't just regular zombies; they're infected with something else."

As the group made their way towards the hospital, the streets were eerily quiet. The only sounds were the shuffling of their feet and the occasional groan from a zombie. Buck kept his gun at the ready, scanning their surroundings for any signs of danger.

As they rounded a corner, they saw the hospital in the distance. It was surrounded by a horde of zombies, their arms outstretched and moaning hungrily.

"We're going to have to go in there," Buck said grimly.

Cassie looked at him with concern. "Are you sure that's a good idea? There's so many of them."

"We don't have a choice," Buck replied. "If we want to stop this thing, we need to find out what caused it and how to stop it."

They approached the hospital slowly, careful not to draw too much attention to themselves. As they got closer, they could see that the building had been fortified with barricades and barbed wire.

"This doesn't look good," Cassie whispered.

Buck nodded in agreement. "We'll have to find a way in."

They circled around the perimeter of the hospital, looking for a weak spot in the defenses. Finally, they found an unlocked door at the back of the building.

As they entered the hospital, they were hit with a wave of putrid smells and moans. The fluorescent lights flickered overhead as they made their way down the hallway, guns at the ready.

Suddenly, they heard a scream from one of the rooms. They rushed towards it, bursting through the door to find a nurse being attacked by a zombie.

Hospital.

The group enters the hospital.

Soldiers are seen patrolling the floor.

Buck: "Hey soldier."

Sgt McGuire: "Yeah?"

Buck: "The only way to kill them is to shoot them in the head or destroy the brain."

Sgt McGuire: "How do you know?"

Buck: "Because we killed a lot of them at the cemetery."

Sgt McGuire: "Okay thanks."

The soldiers get into a battle with zombies on the 6th floor.

Zombies line the halls on the 7th 8th and 9th floors.

Buck: "Lets search each floor one room at a time."

The group searches the 1st floor one room at a time but don't find any zombies.

More soldiers arrive at the hospital.

The soldiers kill all the zombies on the 6th 7th 8th and 9th floors.

The group searches the 2nd floor one room at a time and kill 6 zombies.

The soldiers are seen celebrating victory.

The group searches the 3rd floor one room at a time and kill 20 zombies.

The soldiers search the 5th floor and kill 75 zombies.

The group searches the 4th floor one room at a time and kill 50 zombies.

The soldiers meet with the group to find out if it's clear.

Sgt McGuire: "Did you clear each floor?"

Buck: "Yes, the only floor we didn't find any zombies on was the first."

Sgt McGuire: Laughs and says "That's because we cleared the first floor before you got here."

Sally May: "Did you search the basement?"

Sgt McGuire: "I didn't know there was a basement."

Sally May: " All hospitals have a basement."

Sgt McGuire: "It's not on the floor plan they gave us."

Buck: "Can I see the floor plan?"

Sgt McGuire gives the floor plan to Buck.

Buck: "Shit, this is an old floor plan. According to this we're in the elevator shaft. This is from the old building so it's no good. I think I can find the basement."

The soldiers and the group walk back down to the 1st floor.

The 1st floor is lined with hundreds of zombies.

Buck: What the fuck? I thought we all cleared the 1st floor."

Sgt McGuire: "We did."

Buck: "Then where the hell did all of these damn zombies come from?"

Sally May: "This is just a guess but I'm gonna say they came up from the basement."

The soldiers and the group kill the zombies.

Buck: "Think there are more of them in the basement?"

Sgt McGuire: "Probably."

Buck: "Lets save ourselves the trouble of having to chase dead people in the dark and just demolish the hospital."

Sgt McGuire: "Good idea."

The group leaves the hospital.

The soldiers leave the hospital.

Buck shoots the hospital with 5 rpgs causing it to collapse.

Bubba: "I feel sorry for the poor bastard that has to clean that up."

Cletus: "I'm hungry, lets go to the grocery store."

The group goes to the grocery store.

As the group enters the grocery store, they are met with a gruesome sight. Blood and guts are splattered across the walls, and the floor is littered with body parts. Buck raises his gun, ready to fire at any living dead that may be lurking in the store.

Sally May: "Oh my god, what happened here?"

Buck: "Looks like there was a fight. And it wasn't with the living."

Cletus: "Are there any supplies left?"

Bubba searches through the remains of the store and comes back with a few cans of food and a bottle of water. The group huddles together, taking a moment to rest and regain their strength.

Buck: "We need to keep moving. We can't stay in one place for too long. Who knows what's out there."

As they make their way through the aisles, they hear a faint groaning noise. They follow the sound to one of the back rooms of the store. Inside, they find a young man, barely conscious and covered in bite marks.

Buck: "We need to put him out of his misery."

Sally May: "No! We can save him!"

Buck: "He's already turned. We can't risk having him turn on us."

Sally May refuses to leave him behind. The group debates about what to do with him before ultimately deciding to take him with them.

As they leave the grocery store, they hear more groaning noises echoing throughout the abandoned streets. The group braces themselves for what's to come next - they must fight for their survival against both zombies and other survivors who may be violent.

As they made their way to the grocery store, Buck couldn't help but wonder how many other buildings in the city were infested with zombies. He knew it was only a matter of time before they stumbled upon another hive of them. The thought made his skin crawl.

When they arrived at the grocery store, they found that it had already been picked clean by other survivors. All that was left were a few canned goods and some stale bread. Buck let out a sigh. This was going to be a long night.

Suddenly, they heard a loud crash coming from the back of the store. Buck motioned for everyone to stay put as he crept towards the noise, his rifle at the ready.

As he turned the corner, he saw a sight that made him freeze in horror. A group of survivors had been trapped under a pile of rubble caused by an explosion. It was obvious that they had been scavenging for supplies when something had gone wrong.

Without hesitating, Buck ran towards them and began to pull away the debris. The others followed suit, and soon they had freed the trapped survivors.

As they helped them to their feet, Buck realized with relief that none of them were infected. They were just like him, just trying to survive in this new reality.

The leader of the group introduced himself as Tom and thanked Buck and his team for saving them. In return, Tom offered to join forces with them in their search for safety.

Buck looked around at his team, seeing their fatigue and desperation etched on their faces. "Welcome aboard," he said with a grin.

As the group entered the grocery store, they could hear the shrill moans of the undead that had been lurking inside. Buck raised his shotgun to his shoulder and led the group forward, his eyes scanning the aisles for movement.

The first zombie they encountered was a little girl, no more than ten years old. Her skin was gray and rotting, her eyes clouded over with death. Buck hesitated for a moment, but the little girl was already upon him before he could react. He pulled the trigger and her head exploded in a shower of gore.

Sally May looked away, holding back a gag as Buck turned to face her. "Sorry," he muttered. "She was already gone."

The group moved through the aisles slowly, searching each shelf for supplies. Canned foods, dried goods, bottled water. Buck grabbed an armful of supplies and carried them over to the cart.

Suddenly there was a loud crash from the other side of the store. The group froze, listening intently as something big and heavy moved through the debris.

Cletus cocked his rifle. "What do you think it is?"

Buck shook his head. "I don't know, but we better be ready."

Slowly, they moved towards the noise. As they got closer, they could see a massive figure standing in front of a toppled shelf.

It was a zombie, but this one was different from any they'd seen before. It must have been over eight feet tall and weighed at least 300 pounds, with thick muscles bulging under its rotting flesh.

As the group enters the grocery store, they are met with an unexpected sight. The once clean and tidy store has been ransacked, with shelves overturned and food scattered everywhere. It is obvious that the store had already been looted before they arrived.

Sally May: "Damn, looks like we aren't the only ones who had the idea to come here."

Buck: "We still might be able to find something useful. Split up and search the store."

As Buck and Sally May search one aisle, they hear a noise coming from behind them. Turning around, they see a zombie shuffling towards them.

Buck: "Shit, there's a zombie!"

Sally May quickly pulls out her machete and charges at the zombie. A quick swing of her blade severs its head from its neck.

Sgt McGuire: "We can't stay here for too long, we need to keep moving."

As they make their way through the store, Bubba spots something in one of the freezers.

Bubba: "Hey, guys! I found a bunch of frozen meat back here!"

Cletus rushes over to join him.

Cletus: "Yeehaw! We hit the jackpot!"

As they begin loading up their bags with the frozen meat, another group of survivors enters the store.

Survivor 1: "Hey! What are you doing?! That was our loot!"

Survivor 2: "Get out of here before we make you leave!"

Buck steps forward, his hand resting on the handle of his gun.

Buck: "You might want to think twice before you do anything stupid."

Grocery Store.

The group enters the store.

2 zombies are seen racing shopping carts.

The butcher is seen putting human heads in the meat locker.

Buck: "Guys, I don't think this is where we can find food."

Bubba: "Why?'

Buck: "We don't eat people."

The butcher is seen chasing people thru the store with a meat clever.

The zombies see the group and say "Fresh meat."

The group run out of the store.

Buck plants C4 on the door and as they walk away he detonates it causing the store to explode.

Buck: "Lets go to the gun shop."

The group goes to the gun shop.

As they walked towards the gun shop, Buck couldn't help but think how he should have known better than to venture into a shady store like that. He had seen enough horror movies to know what could happen in situations like that. He wasn't quite sure where they were headed, but he knew they needed to be armed if they were going to survive the apocalypse.

The gun shop was located on the outskirts of town, next to an old gas station. They approached the entrance, and Bubba tried to open the door, but it was locked. He turned around and shrugged at the group.

Suddenly, a voice from inside the shop yelled, "Who's there?" The group looked at each other and then back at the door.

Buck stepped forward and announced, "We need guns. We're looking for anything that will help us against those things out there."

The door slowly creaked open, revealing a tall man with greasy hair and a scraggly beard. His yellow smile revealed missing teeth and Buck wondered if the man was even sober.

The man looked them up and down before saying, "You got any cash?"

Buck pulled out his wallet and handed a few crumpled bills to the man.

The shopkeeper took the money and gestured towards the shelves filled with various guns and ammunition.

"Take your pick," he said with a grin.

Bubba eagerly grabbed a shotgun from the rack, while Lily found a handgun that felt comfortable in her hand. Buck hesitated for a moment before selecting an assault rifle.

As they made their way back outside, they heard a commotion coming from behind them.

As they approached the gun store, they could hear the sound of gunshots echoing in the distance. Buck was getting nervous, but he knew they had to press on if they wanted to survive.

As they entered the store, the group was greeted by an unsettling sight. Bodies lay scattered across the floor, with blood and bullet holes covering every surface. It was apparent that a fierce battle had taken place here, and whoever had been fighting wasn't taking any prisoners.

Buck cautiously stepped over a fallen shelf, scanning the aisles for any sign of danger. Suddenly, a hand shot out from behind a display case, grabbing Buck's ankle and pulling him down to the ground.

Panicking, Buck quickly aimed his pistol at his assailant - but froze when he saw who it was. The man before him was pale and thin, with sunken eyes and a gaunt expression that suggested he hadn't eaten in days.

"It's okay," whispered the man. "I won't hurt you. I'm just looking for food."

Buck hesitated, but something in the man's voice made him lower his weapon. He extended a hand to help the man up, and as they stood face to face, Buck realized that this survivor was more like him than he had originally thought.

Together, they scoured the shelves for supplies, loading up on ammo and weapons as they went. They worked together seamlessly, moving in sync as they loaded up their bags with everything they needed to stay alive.

As they made their way towards the exit of the store, Buck couldn't help but feel grateful for this chance encounter. In this new world, it can be hard to make friends, or even have any reason to feel even the smallest sliver of happiness or hope.

As they walk towards the gun shop, their footsteps echoed on the deserted street. The sun was setting, casting long shadows on the cracked pavement. Bubba nervously adjusts his backpack, he's been feeling paranoid ever since they entered the city. He shudders at the thought of being trapped in the store with the butcher and the zombies.

Suddenly, a hissing sound is heard from behind them. They turn around to see a zombie sneaking up on them. Buck quickly pulls out his pistol and shoots it in the head. The zombie falls to the ground lifeless.

"Thanks," Bubba says, wiping sweat from his forehead.

"No problem," Buck replies with a grin. He leads them towards the gun shop, which was located in a small alley. They slow down when they see that the alley is blocked by a pile of debris.

Buck takes out his pocketknife and starts cutting through the pile. After a few minutes of hard work, they manage to clear a passage and enter the gun shop.

Inside, they find themselves surrounded by rows and rows of weapons; rifles, pistols, shotguns, machine guns - every kind of weapon imaginable. The group marvels at all the firepower available to them.

Suddenly, they hear a sound from behind one of the shelves. They look at each other nervously and reach for their weapons. Buck slowly walks over to investigate and finds a man cowering in fear.

"Don't shoot!" the man cries out, holding up his hands in surrender. Buck approaches him cautiously. "Who are you?"

The man introduces himself as Dave, a survivor from another group that was overrun by zombies

As they approached the gun shop, they saw that the entrance was barricaded with a pile of dead bodies. The group hesitated, but they knew they needed weapons to survive. Buck took out his shotgun and began to shoot the pile of bodies until a hole had been made big enough for them to climb through.

Once inside, they were greeted by the stench of gunpowder and death. The shelves had been picked clean, but there were still a few guns left scattered around the store. They quickly grabbed what they could find - a couple of pistols, rifles and shotguns - and loaded up on ammunition.

Suddenly, they heard shuffling coming from the back room. They cautiously approached, guns in hand. As they entered the room, they were greeted by a group of survivors who had also sought refuge in the gun shop.

One of them, a woman with short blonde hair named Sarah, stepped forward. "We've been hiding in here for days," she said. "We thought we were the only ones left."

Bubba stepped up beside Buck. "We're headed to Washington D.C. to try and find a cure," he said.

Sarah shook her head. "We tried that already," she replied. "The government has fallen, and there's no hope left."

Buck stepped forward, his shotgun still in hand. "We can't just give up like that," he said firmly.

Sarah looked at him with tears in her eyes. "I lost my family to this virus," she said. "I don't want to lose anyone else."

Gun Shop.

The group enters the gun shop.

Buck: "Where's the owner?"

Sally May: "Probably dead."

Buck: "Oh well , get all of the weapons and ammo and load it on the truck."

The group loads all of the weapons and ammo on the truck and they leave.

The gun shop owner walks out of the back and looks around and says " Where did everything go?"

As the group drove off with their new spoils, they rejoiced at the amount of firepower they had just acquired. Guns, ammunition, and explosives; all of it would come in handy in the coming days. Buck, the leader of the group, had a plan in mind and the weapons they had just acquired were a key factor in its success.

As they drove on, Sally May suddenly spoke up, "We need to find someplace safe to stash all of this. It's not like we can keep it in plain sight." The rest of the group nodded in agreement but Buck was quiet. His mind was already racing ahead, making plans for how to use all of their new weapons.

It wasn't until they had reached a secluded cabin deep in the woods that Buck finally spoke up. "Alright everyone, listen up. Here's what we're gonna do..."

The group spent hours strategizing and planning out their next steps. It was clear that they were gearing up for something big and dangerous. But as night fell and they all settled into their makeshift beds, the gun shop owner was still standing there in shock, trying to make sense of what had just happened.

Little did he know that his life was about to be turned upside down as he unwittingly became a part of Buck's dangerous plan.

As the group drove away, they felt a sense of relief wash over them. They had finally found a place with enough weapons and ammo to survive in this post-apocalyptic world. Sally May was in charge of the inventory and began to sort through the weapons they had acquired.

"Hey Buck, come take a look at these," she called out. "I found some pretty interesting pieces."

Buck walked over to her and looked at the assortment of weapons on display. They had everything from pistols, shotguns, and rifles to grenades and rocket launchers.

"Damn, we hit the jackpot," Buck said with a grin. "We'll be able to take on anything that comes our way now."

As they continued down the road, they heard a loud noise coming from the back of the truck. They pulled over and got out to investigate.

"What the hell is going on back there?" Buck asked as he opened the truck door.

To their surprise, they found the gun shop owner hiding in the back of the truck amongst all the weapons and ammo.

"Well, well, well," Buck said with a smirk. "Looks like someone wanted to hitch a ride with us."

The gun shop owner trembled in fear as Buck and Sally May towered over him.

"What do we do with him?" Sally May asked.

Buck thought for a moment before responding. "Either he joins us or he dies."

The gun shop owner hesitated before nodding his head in agreement. From that point on, he was part of their group – providing them with valuable knowledge about weapons and tactics.

As the group drove away in their truck, the sun began to set on the horizon. They had just left the small town of Millford, where they had been hiding out for the past few weeks. Buck and Sally May were leading a small band of survivors on the run from a group of bandits that had been terrorizing their community.

They needed weapons and ammunition to fight back against their attackers, and the gun shop in Millford was their best bet. Buck had always been a bit rough around the edges, but he was a born leader and knew how to get what he wanted.

As they drove down the deserted road, they heard a noise coming from the back of the truck. Sally May turned to look and saw that one of the boxes had fallen over and spilled some of its contents onto the floor.

She climbed over the seats to take a closer look and saw that it was a box of grenades. She picked one up and examined it carefully, feeling its weight in her hand.

Suddenly, she heard footsteps approaching from behind. She spun around just in time to see the gun shop owner standing there with a look of anger on his face.

"Put that down!" he shouted.

Sally May hesitated for a second before dropping the grenade back into the box.

"What are you doing?" Buck demanded, his hand on his gun.

The gun shop owner held up his hands in surrender. "Look, I don't want any trouble," he said. "I just want to know what's going on."

Buck eyed him suspiciously before lowering his weapon. "We needed those weapons to protect ourselves," he explained.

But as he looked around, the gun shop owner noticed something odd. There was no sign of a break-in. Everything seemed to be in place, except for the weapons and ammo that had just vanished into thin air.

He looked at the CCTV footage, and couldn't believe his eyes. There were five people who had entered the store, grabbing everything they could get their hands on. One of them was even wearing a cowboy hat.

The gun shop owner recognized them right away. They were the notorious Wild West gang, known for their daring robberies and deadly shootouts. He knew he had to act fast if he wanted to recover his valuable merchandise and bring these outlaws to justice.

He quickly called the sheriff's office and reported the theft. The sheriff promised him that they would do everything in their power to catch the gang and recover the stolen goods.

Meanwhile, Buck and his gang were celebrating their successful heist. They had enough guns and ammo to last them a lifetime. They were already planning their next robbery when suddenly, they heard police sirens in the distance.

They quickly realized that they were being pursued by law enforcement. Buck ordered his gang to split up and meet at a predetermined location later on, hoping that it would throw off the cops' pursuit.

As Buck raced through town in his truck with the stolen weapons, he couldn't help but feel a rush of excitement. He loved living life on the edge, always on the run from the law.

But little did he know that the gun shop owner had tipped off the police about their whereabouts. The Wild West gang was about to experience a shootout like never before.

Back on the farm.

Buck: "Lets go back to the farm at least there we're on our own turf."

The group goes back to the farm.

Bubba: "Okay , now what?"

Buck: "Lets hunt some dead people."

The group is seen driving around the farm killing zombies.

Zombies are seen on every farm in the area.

The group drives around and kill the zombies.

Buck: "Lets park the truck by the gun shed and hunt them on horse back."

The group parks the truck by the gun shed.

As they make their way to the stables, Buck can't help but feel a sense of exhilaration. Hunting zombies on horseback was something he had always dreamed about, and now, in the midst of the apocalypse, it was finally happening.

Buck saddles up his trusty stallion, Thunder, and hands a horse to each member of the group. They all mount up, armed with crossbows and machetes.

The sun is setting in a brilliant array of oranges and pinks as they begin their hunt. The fields are choked with weeds and dead crops, and the smell of decay is heavy in the air. But Buck barely notices. He's too focused on the thrill of the chase.

They come across a small group of zombies stumbling through a field. Buck signals for everyone to spread out and take aim. The horses prance nervously beneath them, sensing the danger ahead.

With a cry, Buck charges forward, Thunder's powerful muscles propelling them towards the group of undead. He swings his machete, slicing through the air and decapitating one zombie before it even has a chance to react.

The others follow suit, crossbows firing and blades flashing. The horses dance around the zombies, nimble and quick on their feet.

For hours they ride, hunting down any zombie in their path. It's dangerous work, but Buck loves every moment of it. He feels more alive than he has in weeks.

As the moon rises high in the sky, signaling the end of their hunt, Buck can't help but feel a sense of accomplishment. They've made their farm just a little bit safer tonight, and that's no easy task.

As they approached the shed, Buck reached into the back of the truck and grabbed a couple of shotguns. He handed one to Bubba and kept one for himself. They then walked towards the stable, where they found a couple of horses.

"Alright boys, let's saddle up," Buck said in a low tone.

The group mounted their horses and rode towards the field where they had spotted a herd of zombies from the truck. As they rode past the cornfields, Buck noticed that one of the zombies was different from the others. It was bigger, stronger, and faster.

"Guys, take out the normal ones first. Leave the big one to me," Buck ordered.

The three men split up and began picking off zombies one by one. The sound of gunshots echoed through the empty countryside as Buck approached the larger zombie. It snarled and lunged at him with incredible speed, but Buck was ready. He quickly aimed his shotgun and fired a round directly into its head. The zombie fell to the ground with a thud.

Buck turned towards Bubba with a grin on his face. "Looks like our hunt just got interesting," he said.

The group continued riding through the farmland, taking out any zombies that crossed their path. As they rode together under the bright moonlight, Buck couldn't help but feel alive. This was what he had been born to do - hunt and kill zombies.

After several hours of riding, they returned to the farm where they began to unload their weapons. As they cleaned their shotguns, Buck turned towards Bubba.

"You know, this was a good night," Buck said.

They walk inside the shed and look at the rifles on the racks. Buck hands Bubba a shotgun and grabs a hunting rifle for himself. They exit the shed to find three horses tied up outside. Buck assigns each member of the group to their respective horse.

As they ride through the fields, they spot a group of zombies in the distance. Buck signals for everyone to slow down and get closer. He motions to Bubba to take out the first zombie, which he does with ease. The other zombies start to notice the commotion and begin to charge towards them.

Buck leads the charge on his horse, firing his rifle as he goes. The rest of the group follows suit, taking out any zombie that comes too close. The horses are spooked by the undead and start to buck, but Buck calms them down with a quick pat and a reassuring voice.

The group rides around for hours, taking out as many zombies as they can find. Just as they are about to call it a day, they hear a faint cry for help in the distance. Without hesitation, Buck leads his group towards the sound.

As they near the source of the noise, they see a young woman being attacked by a group of zombies. Buck jumps off his horse and rushes towards her with his rifle in hand. He takes out the first two zombies with ease and signals for Bubba to take care of the rest.

The woman is grateful and introduces herself as Sarah. She explains that she was trying to find her family's farm when she was ambushed by the undead. Buck invites her to join their group since she's alone in this apocalypse.

Bubba helps Buck saddle up the horses and they all mount up, armed to the teeth and ready to hunt some zombies. As they ride out into the fields, they can hear the groans of the undead in the distance.

Samantha takes point, her keen eyes scanning the horizon for any signs of movement. She spots a small group of zombies shuffling towards them, and signals to the rest of the group to follow her lead.

They ride towards the undead, guns blazing, swords flashing in the sunlight. The zombies try to swarm them, but the group works together seamlessly, mowing them down with ease.

As they ride through the countryside, picking off zombies left and right, a strange sensation washes over Bubba. He feels alive in a way he hasn't felt in years, exhilarated by the thrill of the hunt.

Samantha notices his newfound energy and grins at him. "Looks like we've got ourselves a real cowboy here," she says with a laugh.

Bubba chuckles and nods. "I guess so," he replies. "Who knew killing zombies could be so damn fun?"

The group continues their hunt well into the night, taking down wave after wave of zombies without breaking a sweat. When they finally return to the farm at dawn, exhausted but satisfied, Buck claps Bubba on the back.

"Looks like we've found ourselves a new hobby," he says with a grin. "Welcome to the club."

Hunting on horseback.

The group is seen riding thru the nearby farms looking for zombies.

Zombies are seen hiding from the group.

The group continues riding.

Zombies run out in front of the group.

The group kills the zombies.

Buck: "Even for dead people that was a dumb move. Especially since those dead people spend all of their time eating brains. You would think they would be smarter than that."

Brutus: "Yeah but you have to remember most of those dead people were drop outs so you can't expect them to be very smart."

Buck: "I guess one thing is true that you see in movies."

Cletus: "What's that?"

Buck: "Dead people are stupid."

The group continues riding.

As they rode on, the sun began to set and the sky turned a deep shade of orange. The fields around them stretched for miles, dotted with small clusters of trees. Despite the endless farmland, there was a deep sense of loneliness that hung in the air. They were the only ones out here, hunting down those who had already died.

Suddenly, Ralph let out a shout. "Look! Over there!" he cried out, pointing towards a small shack in the distance. The others looked over and saw what he was talking about - there were dozens of zombies heading towards the small building.

"We've got to help them!" shouted Brutus, urging his horse forward.

The group rode towards the shack, their horses closing in on the zombies from behind. Before the undead could even react, Cletus was upon them. With a swift flick of his wrist, he drew his sword and sliced through their ranks.

The rest of the group followed suit, cutting down zombie after zombie with incredible speed and precision. It was like watching a well-oiled machine at work - each member of the group moved with perfect coordination, taking out their targets with ease.

After a few minutes of intense fighting, the last zombie fell to the ground at their feet. The group paused for a moment to catch their breaths before turning back towards the shack.

As they drew closer, they saw an older man emerge from the building. He was ruggedly dressed and had a gruff look about him, but there was a softness in his eyes that betrayed a kind soul.

"Thank you," he said simply as he approached them. "I thought I was done for."

Suddenly, they hear a loud growling sound. It's not the moaning of zombies, but something else entirely. They look around, scanning the area for any signs of danger.

As they round a bend in the road, they come face to face with a massive grizzly bear. Its fur is matted with blood and it has a crazed look in its eyes. It charges towards them, ready to pounce.

Buck and Brutus both draw their guns and begin firing at the bear. But their bullets seem to have no effect. The bear keeps coming, getting closer and closer.

Cletus looks around frantically for some sort of escape route. But there's nowhere to go. They're surrounded by farmland and open fields. The bear is almost upon them now.

Just when it seems like all hope is lost, a figure appears from out of nowhere. It's a woman dressed in leather armor and wielding a massive sword. She charges towards the bear, her sword raised high.

The group watches in amazement as she slices through the bear with ease. The beast falls to the ground, dead.

The woman turns towards the group, a fierce look on her face. "You're lucky I was passing by," she says. "That bear would have made short work of you."

Buck steps forward, his gun still in hand. "Who are you?" he asks.

The woman sheaths her sword and smiles faintly. "I'm just passing through," she says, before disappearing into the nearby woods.

The group is left standing there, stunned by what they've just witnessed. They continue riding, their minds racing.

As they rode through the empty streets, the sun had begun to set, casting an orange and purple glow over the town. In the distance, they could hear the faint sounds of groaning and shuffling coming from a nearby cemetery. It didn't take long for the group to realize that the zombies they had killed earlier were just a small taste of what was to come.

"We should check out that cemetery," suggested Brutus. "We might find some useful supplies and weapons."

Buck nodded in agreement. "Alright, but be careful. The dead might be smarter than we think."

The group dismounted their horses and slowly made their way towards the cemetery gate. As they pushed open the rusted iron gate, they were met with a cloud of dust and decay.

Cletus wrinkled his nose in disgust. "Damn, it smells worse than my uncle's moonshine!"

As they made their way deeper into the graveyard, they noticed that several of the tombstones had been broken and knocked over. Suddenly, they heard a low growling noise coming from behind them.

They turned around to see a pack of zombies stumbling towards them, drawn by the sound of their horses. Buck quickly took out his shotgun and fired a shot, taking down two of them.

Brutus and Cletus drew their machetes and plunged them into the skulls of several more zombies. But as they continued fighting off the undead, more and more began to emerge from the shadows.

It wasn't long before the group found themselves completely surrounded by the flesh-eating monsters with no escape route. Buck cursed under his breath as he prepared for what he thought would be their last stand.

As they rode through the abandoned farmland, the sky darkened and a low growl could be heard in the distance. The group slowed their pace and exchanged nervous glances.

Suddenly, without warning, a pack of zombies rushed towards them. Buck drew his pistol and shot them down one by one. Their brains exploded in a shower of gore as they fell to the ground.

Cletus couldn't help but feel impressed. "Nice shooting, Buck."

But as they continued down the dirt road, more zombies appeared from every direction. The group was soon surrounded, with no clear way out.

Brutus drew his machete and charged forward, slicing through limbs and heads as he went. Buck fired round after round, but there were simply too many of them.

As the situation became increasingly dire, Cletus reached for something in his bag. With a sly grin, he pulled out a grenade.

"Guys," he shouted over the din of snarling zombies. "I think I've got just the thing!"

Without waiting for their protests, Cletus pulled the pin and hurled it into the midst of their attackers. As the explosion shook the ground beneath them, the group watched in awe as the zombies were sent flying in every direction.

When they finally caught their breath and looked around at the carnage they had wrought, Buck chuckled ruefully. "Well," he said. "At least we know dead people are still stupid."

Zombies eating animal brains.

Animals are seen running thru the woods.

Zombies are seen chasing animals.

Animals are seen chasing zombies.

Zombies are seen eating animals.

Animals are seen eating zombies.

Zombies are seen eating animal brains.

The eerie scene in the woods only intensified as the zombie hoard continued their relentless pursuit of the terrified animals. The sound of snapping branches and panicked breaths filled the air, as the creatures raced through the forest.

But suddenly, a strange shift occurred. The animals, desperate to escape their brain-hungry pursuers, began to fight back. The smaller creatures nipped and bit at the zombies' heels, distracting them just enough for larger beasts to charge in and take them down.

The zombies were no match for the fierce determination of the animal kingdom. In a turn of events that nobody could have predicted, it was now the zombies who were running scared. The creatures tore into their decaying flesh with wild abandon, tearing off limbs and devouring them whole.

As the last of the zombies fell to their ravenous jaws, a sense of peace settled over the woods once more. But for how long? Who knew what other terrors lurked in these dark corners, waiting to pounce on unsuspecting prey? One thing was certain - life would never be quite the same again in this cursed corner of the world.

The scene in the woods was chaos. The animals ran for their lives, senses heightened as they darted between trees, jumped over bushes, and swam through creeks. They were running from the zombies, who were chasing them with a relentless hunger burning in their eyes.

But then something strange happened. The deer at the front of the pack suddenly stopped and turned around. The zombies slowed as they approached, snarling and licking their lips in anticipation of their meal. But the deer didn't run away; instead, it charged straight at the zombies.

The other animals soon followed suit. Wolves, foxes, raccoons, even rodents - all of them ran towards the zombies, teeth bared and claws extended. Chaos turned into a battle as the two sides collided.

The zombies were taken by surprise at first, but then they fought back with equal ferocity. They ripped into the animals with teeth and nails, tearing flesh from bone and leaving corpses scattered on the ground.

But even in death, the animals continued to fight back. Strange energy seemed to surge through their bodies as they rose again, eyes glowing with an otherworldly light as they attacked the zombies once more.

The zombies weren't just after flesh, it seemed. They craved something more - something that only animal brains could provide. They eagerly gorged on the skulls of their prey, relishing in the taste of raw meat and blood.

The woods were now a battlefield unlike any other - a place where beasts fought against monsters for survival. And through it all, a strange feeling simmered beneath the surface - a feeling that maybe, just maybe, there was something deeper

The forest was alive with a frenzied energy that refused to settle. A pack of wolves ran through the woods, their fur ruffling against the cold wind. Behind them, a group of zombies followed, their rotting feet pounding against the frozen earth.

The wolves ran with a frantic grace, their eyes scanning the surroundings for any possible escape route. They moved in perfect coordination, zigzagging through the trees and over fallen branches. But the zombies were relentless, driven by a hunger that could not be satiated. They stumbled and fell, but always picked themselves up again, driven by some primal force.

And then something strange happened.

One of the wolves suddenly stopped and turned around. It bared its sharp teeth, growling at the zombie that was slowly closing in on it. And then, to everyone's surprise, it leaped forward and attacked.

At first, the zombie seemed taken aback, unsure of how to respond. But then it rallied and tried to fight back, clawing at the wolf's fur with its decaying hands. The other zombies watched in silence as they saw the wolf sink its teeth into the zombie's neck.

But even as they watched this gruesome spectacle unfold, they did not realize that something else was happening in those woods. Something that was far more dangerous than any zombie or wolf.

Deep in the forest, there was an ancient evil stirring - an entity that had been awakened from its slumber by all the chaos and bloodshed. And now it hungered for something more than just animal brains. It wanted human flesh.

As the pack of wolves and zombies continued their deadly dance through the woods, they were

The sight of animals running through the woods was now a common occurrence, with the undead roaming around, terrorizing the natural order. In this post-apocalyptic world, nature had become unpredictable and twisted. As she ran through the dense forest, Grace could hear the sound of zombies growling and chasing after the animals.

Grace could see a group of deer in front of her, frantically fleeing from a pack of zombies. She paused for a moment to catch her breath. Suddenly, she heard something behind her. She turned around to see a zombie chasing after her. Grace sprinted as fast as she could, desperate to escape.

As she ran, she noticed that some of the smaller animals were now chasing after the zombies. She saw a pack of coyotes circling around a group of zombies, nipping at their heels. The world had turned upside down in every sense imaginable.

Grace could see that some of the larger animals had even resorted to eating the zombies. A group of bears tore apart a zombie that had stumbled into their territory. The crunching sound echoed throughout the forest.

In turn, some of the zombies had developed a taste for animal brains. They would attack any animal they came across just for one bite of brain.

Grace wasn't sure how much longer she would be able to survive in this world. But as long as nature continued to adapt and evolve in such strange ways, there was always hope.

Zombies on ATVs.

The group is seen riding thru the woods.

5 zombies are seen riding atvs toward the group.

Buck: " Hey look at the dead people on atvs."

The zombies ride along side of the group and say "Who's stupid now? The rednecks on horses or the zombies that are gonna eat the rednecks?"

Buck: "Actually , you're still stupid."

Zombies: "Why?"

The group shoots the zombies.

Buck: "We have guns."

The group continues riding.

A zombie tries to chase the group on an atv but it crashes into a tree before they saw it.

As the group continued riding through the woods, Buck couldn't help but feel a sense of unease. They had encountered zombies before, but seeing them on ATVs was a new level of unsettling.

Just as he was lost in thought, a loud crash startled him back to reality. One of the zombies that had been chasing them had crashed into a tree. Buck felt a sense of relief wash over him - at least for now, they were safe.

But moments later, a shrill scream pierced through the woods. It was one of their own - Anne. Buck's heart raced as he spurred his horse into action, galloping towards the source of the sound.

As he approached, he saw Anne surrounded by a group of zombies. They were closing in fast, and Anne was frantically trying to fend them off with her crossbow.

Buck quickly pulled out his revolver and took aim. He fired off three shots, taking down two of the zombies. But just as he pulled the trigger for the third time, his gun jammed.

He cursed under his breath as he tried to fix it, but it was too late. The remaining zombie lunged towards Anne and sank its teeth into her neck.

Buck watched in horror as his friend's body convulsed and went limp. He knew there was no coming back from that kind of bite.

With tears in his eyes, he drew his machete and charged towards the zombie horde. It was time to show those undead bastards that they weren't going down without a fight.

As the group rode through the dense forest, they were careful to stay alert at all times. The sight of zombies on ATVs had been a surprise, but it wasn't enough to stop them from moving forward. They continued to ride along as if nothing had happened, but the encounter had left them feeling uneasy.

Suddenly, Buck noticed movement in the corner of his eye. He turned his head just in time to see a zombie speeding towards them on an ATV. Buck couldn't help but feel a sense of amusement at the thought of a zombie riding an ATV. However, their humor was short-lived as the zombie began to shout insults at them.

But Buck's response was quick as he brought his gun up and aimed it unapologetically at the zombie. The others followed suit and quickly disposed of the approaching undead. Meanwhile, the remaining zombies were thrown off guard by this sudden attack and became hesitant.

"Looks like we're still smarter than you," Buck said with a smirk before they all continued on their journey.

As they rode off, they could hear one of the zombies try to chase them down on another ATV. However, luck seemed to be on their side as the zombie lost control and crashed into a nearby tree.

The group laughed as they watched the zombie fall off its vehicle and onto the ground, wriggling around in pain. For a moment, they felt a sense of relief knowing that they could overcome any obstacle thrown their way - even if it meant fighting off zombies on ATVs. But deep down inside, they knew that this was just another day in their new post-apocalyptic world.

As they rode deeper into the woods, the group began to feel a sense of unease. The trees grew thicker, casting an ominous shadow over their path. Buck rode at the front of the group, his shotgun loaded and ready.

Suddenly, they heard the sound of engines in the distance. At first, they thought it might be another group of survivors. But as the noise grew closer, they realized it was something far more sinister.

Five zombies emerged from the trees, riding ATVs and hurtling towards them at breakneck speed. Buck cursed under his breath.

"Hey look at the dead people on ATVs," he said wryly.

The zombies drew level with them, revving their engines menacingly. One of them leaned in close to Buck and sneered:

"Who's stupid now? The rednecks on horses or the zombies that are gonna eat the rednecks?"

Buck didn't hesitate. He lifted his shotgun and fired point blank into the zombie's face.

"Actually, you're still stupid," he said coolly. "Why? Because we have guns."

Within moments, all five zombies lay dead on the forest floor. Buck and the others rode on, their spirits lifted by their victory.

But their elation was short-lived. As they rounded a bend in the path, they saw a lone zombie riding an ATV towards them at full speed. The creature had clearly escaped their notice until now, and it was too late to react.

With a sickening crunch, the zombie crashed into a tree before their eyes. Buck shook his head in disbelief.

"I guess it's true what they say," he mused

As they rode deeper into the woods, the group felt their adrenaline begin to settle. Buck, the de facto leader of the group, looked over at his companions and sighed in relief. They had been lucky so far - lucky to have each other, lucky to have guns and ammo, lucky to have survived this long.

But their luck was about to run out.

As they rounded a bend in the trail, they saw something approaching - something that made their blood run cold.

A pack of wolves, their eyes gleaming in the moonlight, emerged from the shadows.

Buck urged his horse forward, his weapon at the ready. His companions followed suit. The wolves circled around them, growling and snapping their jaws. Buck held his ground, his eyes scanning for any sign of weakness in their attackers.

That's when he noticed something strange.

One of the wolves looked...different. Its fur was matted and dirty, its eyes glassy and vacant. It didn't seem quite as aggressive as the others, almost as if it were under some kind of spell.

Suddenly, the wolf lunged forward, its jaws clamping down on Buck's arm. He screamed in pain as his horse reared up, throwing him to the ground.

His companions rushed forward to defend him, but it was too late - the other wolves had joined in, tearing at flesh and clothing with ferocity.

In moments, everything went black. Buck felt himself slipping away as the wolves devoured him alive. He thought of his loved ones - of all the things he would never get to do again - and then...nothing.

Zombie on a horse.

A zombie is seen riding a horse.

Zombie: " Take me to your people."

Horse: "Are you dead?"

Zombie: "Yes, are you a horse?"

Horse: "Yes, how the devil are you able to walk or talk if you're dead?"

Zombie: "I don't know. How are you able to talk?"

Horse: "I don't know."

Zombie: "Now that we've concluded that we don't know lets find some people, I'm hungry."

Horse: "You eat people?"

Zombie: "Yes."

Horse: "Holy hell." Throws the zombie off of its back and runs away.

The zombie lay there motionless for a while, staring at the sky. He couldn't help but feel a little hurt by the horse's reaction. He wasn't just some mindless monster, he had feelings too. But he knew he couldn't dwell on it for long, he was hungry and needed to find food. Slowly but surely, he got up and started walking.

As he wandered through the countryside, he couldn't help but notice the destruction left in the wake of the undead. Buildings were crumbling, cars abandoned, and all signs of life seemed to have disappeared. The zombie was starting to lose hope when he heard a noise.

Turning around, he saw a human approaching cautiously. The human had a weapon at his side, but didn't seem to be in a hurry to use it. The zombie took a step forward and spoke.

"Take me to your people," he said, his voice raspy from disuse.

The human cautiously approached him, keeping his weapon at the ready. "What are you?" the human asked.

"I'm dead," replied the zombie.

The human seemed surprised at his response. "How are you able to talk?"

"I don't know," said the zombie with a shrug. "But I'm hungry."

The human hesitated for a moment before signaling for the zombie to follow him. Together they walked through the remains of civilization until they reached a group of survivors huddled together in an abandoned building.

The survivors looked warily at the zombie as they approached. The human explained that the zombie had spoken to him and seemed harmless enough. After some deliberation, they decided to let him stay with them

The zombie falls to the ground with a thud, groaning as it hits the dirt. It doesn't fully understand why the horse refused to take it to find more people to devour, but it knows it needs to find sustenance soon. With a growl, the zombie pushes itself up off the ground and starts lumbering forward.

As it walks, its mind is consumed with one thought: finding living flesh to eat. It doesn't notice the trees or the birds or the sunlight streaming through the leaves; all it can focus on is its hunger. It stumbles through the woods for hours, until it finally comes upon a small clearing.

There, sitting around a campfire, are four humans. They're laughing and talking, passing around a bottle of whiskey. The zombie's eyes light up at the sight of them. It stumbles forward, arms outstretched, ready to feast.

The humans scream and scatter as soon as they catch sight of the zombie. One of them trips in their haste to get away, and the zombie pounces on them. Its teeth sink into their flesh with a sickening squelch as it tears off a hunk of muscle.

The other humans watch in horror as their friend is devoured right in front of them. They try to run, but the zombie is too quick for them.

It chases them down one by one, tearing into their flesh until there's nothing left but bones.

As the sun begins to set and the woods grow quiet once again, the zombie sits in the clearing alone. Its belly is full for now, but it knows that hunger will return soon enough.

The zombie lays motionless on the ground for a few moments before standing up to examine its surroundings. It is in the middle of a forest. The zombie realizes that it has no idea how it got here or what it was doing before it met the horse. It tries hard to remember, but its mind is murky.

As it wanders aimlessly through the dense forest, something catches its attention. A faint light in the distance. It shambles towards it, driven by a primal urge to feed.

The light turns out to be a small campfire with two people sitting around it, roasting marshmallows. They don't see the zombie approaching until it's too late. It lunges at them, snarling and gnashing its teeth.

One of the people manages to dodge out of the way and runs for help, leaving the other one behind. But there's nowhere to run in the dark forest, and soon the zombie catches up with him.

As the zombie feeds on his flesh, memories start flooding back into its mind. It remembers being human once, before a virus turned it into a mindless monster. It remembers its name, James, and how it used to love hiking and camping in these very woods.

But now all those memories feel like they belong to someone else, to another world entirely. In this new world, there's only hunger and death and an endless cycle of feeding and killing.

As James finishes his meal and looks around for more victims, he wonders if he'll ever be able to escape this nightmare or if he'll be trapped here forever as a monster among monsters.

The zombie landed with a thud and groaned in frustration. It had lost its mode of transportation, but it wasn't too worried. It had been walking for hours, and it was confident that it would find what it was looking for soon.

As it stumbled down the dusty road, the zombie caught sight of a small cottage nestled at the base of a hill. The windows were dark, but smoke rose from the chimney, indicating that someone was inside.

The zombie approached cautiously, its senses on high alert. As it drew closer to the front door, it could make out some muffled sounds coming from inside. The zombie raised a bony hand and knocked on the door.

There was no response at first, but then a gruff voice called out, "Who's there?"

"I am a traveler seeking shelter," the zombie replied in its raspy voice.

The door creaked open to reveal an old man with a scruffy beard. He peered at the zombie through squinted eyes and said, "You don't look like any traveler I've ever seen."

The zombie shrugged its bony shoulders. "I'm not like most travelers," it said.

The old man wrinkled his nose in distaste. "What do you want?"

"I'm hungry," the zombie said bluntly. "Do you have anything to eat?"

The old man narrowed his eyes suspiciously. "You're not gonna eat me, are you?"

The zombie grinned hungrily. "No promises," it replied.

The old man looked like he was about to slam the door shut when the zombie suddenly lunged forward and sank its teeth into his throat.

Brain eating animals.

The group is seen riding on the road.

Zombie animals run out of the woods toward the group.

Buck: "Oh great brain eating animals."

The group shoot the animals.

More zombie animals run toward the group.

The group shoot the animals.

As the last of the zombie animals fall to the ground, the group lets out a sigh of relief. They had been traveling on this road for days now and they were tired, hungry, and running low on ammunition.

Buck looks over at the newest member of their group, a young woman named Emily. She had joined them a few miles back and was still getting used to the constant danger they faced.

"You alright?" Buck asks, watching as Emily reloads her gun.

Emily nods, "Yeah, just wasn't expecting that."

Buck gives her a small smile, "You'll get used to it."

As they continue down the road, Buck can't shake the feeling that something isn't right. They had been encountering more and more zombie animals lately, but he couldn't figure out why.

Suddenly, they hear a loud growl coming from behind them. They turn around to see a massive zombie bear charging at them.

Buck curses under his breath, "We need to take that thing down before it reaches us!"

The group quickly takes aim and fires at the bear. The bullets ricochet off its thick hide, barely slowing it down.

Realizing that their guns aren't enough to take down the bear, Buck grabs his machete and charges towards it.

The others follow suit and together they engage in a fierce battle with the zombie bear. It's a brutal fight, but eventually they manage to take it down.

Panting heavily, Buck turns to Emily and smiles, "Welcome to the group."

As the last of the zombie animals fell to the ground, Buck let out a sigh of relief. The group had been traveling for weeks, ever since the outbreak had started, and it seemed like everywhere they went there were more and more zombies.

"Is everyone okay?" Buck asked, looking around at his companions. They all nodded, but he could see the exhaustion etched on their faces.

Suddenly, they heard a low growling sound coming from the woods. They all spun around to face the source of the noise, and what they saw made their blood run cold. A pack of zombie wolves emerged from the trees, their eyes glowing red and their jaws dripping with saliva.

"We can't keep doing this," Buck muttered under his breath, as the group raised their weapons once again. "We need to find a safer place to rest."

The pack charged towards them, and the group began firing blindly at them. One by one, the wolves fell to the ground, but there seemed to be an endless number of them.

"We need to move!" Buck shouted over the sounds of gunfire. "Now!"

The group turned and started running down the road as fast as they could, with the pack of zombies hot on their heels. They could hear their ragged panting behind them, feel their hot breath on their necks.

Finally, they saw a small house up ahead and made a mad dash towards it. They slammed the door shut behind them just as the pack reached them, rattling at the doorknob with ferocious snarls.

Buck leaned against the wall, panting heavily. "We need to fortify this place," he demands.

As the group made their way down the deserted road, they could hear the faint growls of the zombie animals lurking in the nearby woods. Buck, their leader, was always prepared for an attack and he quickly signaled to the others to get their weapons ready.

Suddenly, a pack of zombie wolves charged out towards them, their eyes glowing and teeth bared. The group quickly opened fire, shooting down several wolves before they could even reach them. But there were too many of them and more were closing in.

Buck barked out orders to his team, telling them to split into two groups and take down the wolves from both sides. As they moved to execute his plan, Buck noticed a huge zombie moose barreling out from the trees as well. It was unlike anything he had ever seen before.

The massive zombie moose stood taller than any of them, with antlers that looked like they could crush any skull in their path. Buck knew that taking this creature down would be no easy feat.

The group aimed their weapons but nothing seemed to faze the gigantic animal. It continued charging towards them with incredible speed.

With a sudden burst of courage, Buck stepped forward and aimed his shotgun at the moose's head. He steadied his aim and pulled the trigger.

The shot rang out through the forest, echoing off the trees. For a moment, there was silence as everyone held their breath, waiting for something to happen.

And then suddenly, the moose stumbled and crashed to the ground, its massive body convulsing as it let out a final roar before it died.

Buck let out a sigh of relief as he surveyed the surroundings.

As the last of the zombie animals fell to the ground, the group let out a collective sigh of relief. They had been on the road for days, and it seemed like every time they thought they were safe, another group of undead creatures would come at them from out of nowhere.

Buck wiped his forehead with the back of his hand and looked around at his companions. They were all breathing heavily, but no one was hurt.

"We need to be more careful," he said. "We can't keep wasting our ammo like this."

Angie nodded in agreement. "We need to find a safer place to hunker down for a while and restock."

They continued down the road, keeping an eye out for any signs of danger. It wasn't long before they came across an old gas station that looked like it had been abandoned for years.

"Looks like a good place to stop," Buck said as he pulled the van into the parking lot.

They got out and started searching through the shelves, looking for anything they could use. Buck found a bag of beef jerky and tore it open, handing pieces out to everyone.

As they sat there, munching on their snacks, they heard a noise coming from outside. Buck grabbed his gun and motioned for everyone else to stay put.

He slowly made his way to the door and peeked outside. What he saw made him freeze in his tracks.

There were dozens of zombie animals out there, snarling and snapping at each other.

Buck didn't waste any time. He ran back inside and grabbed his companions.

"We have to get out of here now," he shouted.

Zombie on a tractor.

A zombie is seen plowing a field with a huge tractor.

A large woman is seen walking out of her cabin.

The zombie continues to plow the field.

The large woman looks at the zombie and says "Get off my property."

The zombie continues plowing.

The large woman starts walking toward the zombie.

The zombie starts driving toward the woman.

The woman continues walking toward the zombie.

The zombie drives over the woman and says "Yee haw." As pieces of the woman's body fly thru the air.

The sun was just beginning to rise, casting its faint pink-orange hue across the fields, when a figure suddenly emerged from the cabin. It was a large woman, broad shoulders and ample curves hidden beneath a homespun dress, her face barely visible in the growing darkness.

Meanwhile, a few hundred yards away, a huge, mechanical tractor lumbered across a patch of land, churning up the earth with its powerful blades. It was a zombie, its undead movements powering the massive machine as it churned up soil.

The woman watched the zombie with a mix of curiosity and confusion, before finally calling out, her voice ringing across the fields.

"Get off my property!" she shouted, her stern eyes locked on the zombie.

But the zombie paid no mind, continuing on its course, relentlessly plowing.

The woman continued walking, her expression one of determination as she advanced on the zombie. She shouted again, louder this time.

"I said get off my property!"

But the zombie just kept going, getting closer and closer to the woman. It was almost as if it were trying to run her over.

At the last minute, the woman leapt aside just as the zombie drove over her, crashing through the ground. The sound was deafening as pieces of her body flew through the air.

And then, as the dust settled, the zombie stopped. It seemed to pause for a moment before finally coming to a halt. Then it slowly turned its head and, in a deep, raspy voice, spoke the words that would haunt the woman for the rest of her days.

"Yee haw," it said, as it drove off into the night.

Zombie gets snake bit.

Zombies are seen walking through the hills.

A rattle snake is seen crawling through the grass.

The zombies continue walking.

The snake bites a zombie on the butt.

The zombie spins around with the snake attached to his butt.

The other zombies laugh at the zombie with the snake attached to his butt.

The zombie continues spinning around trying to make the snake let go of his butt.

The snake flies through the air.

A zombie is seen eating an arm and gets ready to take a bite and accidently bites the snake.

The snake hisses in anger, but the zombie seems unfazed by the snake's venom. The zombie keeps chewing on the snake, its taste an unexpected surprise. As the other zombies watch in confusion, one by one they start to approach the zombie with the snake in his mouth, intrigued by the sight.

Soon enough, all the zombies gather around the unusual feast, tearing apart the snake and munching on its flesh. They seem to have acquired a new taste for fresh meat and are now on the lookout for other animals to devour.

As they roam through the hills, they come across a group of survivors who are taking refuge in a small cabin. The zombies sense their presence and start to approach, their hunger growing stronger with every step.

The survivors hear the moaning and groaning outside and frantically barricade themselves inside. But it's only a matter of time before the zombies break through their defenses.

As they swarm into the cabin, one of them catches sight of a young woman hiding under a table. He reaches out to grab her but suddenly stops as he catches her scent. She smells different, not like any other human they've ever encountered.

The other zombies gather around her, sniffing and inspecting her curiously. The young woman trembles in fear as she realizes what's happening. She's been bitten by a vampire and has become one herself.

The zombies seem to sense her new identity and back away from her in confusion. She stands up slowly and gazes at them with newfound confidence. She knows she's no longer human but now has the power of the undead on her side.

The snake writhes in pain, coiling around the zombie's arm as he tries to shake it off. The other zombies stop laughing and gather around, their empty eyes fixed on the struggling pair. The bitten zombie groans in anguish, his rotting flesh already weakened by the venom.

As the zombie's strength fades, he slumps to the ground, the snake still clinging to his arm. His undead companions circle him, drawn closer by the smell of fresh blood. One of them reaches out a bony hand and touches the snake, then sniffs its fingers. Without warning, it sinks its teeth into the wriggling reptile.

The other zombies watch in fascination as their comrade tears into the snake, gobbling it down in bite-sized chunks. They too lunge forward, each grabbing a piece of the snake and eagerly devouring it. Soon there is nothing left but a few scraps of sinew and bone.

Satisfied, the zombies shuffle off towards the hills, leaving behind only the carcass of the snake and their fallen brother. As they disappear over the horizon, a faint moaning can be heard on the wind - or is it just the rustle of leaves in the grass?

The snake wriggles in the zombie's mouth, but the undead creature doesn't seem to care. Instead, it chomps down hard, severing the snake's head from its body. The other zombies watch in amazement as the headless snake flops around on the ground.

Meanwhile, the first zombie is still trying to shake off the pain of the snake bite. But something strange is happening. His skin is starting to turn a sickly green color, and his eyes are clouding over.

All of a sudden, he lunges forward and sinks his teeth into another zombie's neck. The bitten zombie roars in pain and tries to fight back, but it's too late. The virus has already taken hold.

The first zombie continues to bite and infect every other undead creature in sight. Soon, all of the zombies in the hills have turned into something even more terrifying - a horde of undead snake-zombies.

They slither through the grass like serpents, their hungry mouths open wide as they search for their next victim. With each bite, the virus spreads further and further, until there's no one left alive to resist it.

For years to come, the world will be plagued by this new breed of zombie. And despite all efforts to eradicate them, they continue to multiply and evolve, adapting to any environment or situation that comes their way.

With every passing day, their numbers grow larger and larger. And soon enough, humanity is nothing more than a distant memory in their decaying minds.

The snake jerks back, sinking its fangs into the zombie's lip. The zombie recoils in pain, flailing its arms and knocking over the other zombies in its frenzy. They all stumble around, tripping and falling into one another.

As they blindly grope for each other, one of the zombies accidentally grabs onto a rattlesnake that's coiled up nearby. It lashes out, biting him on the hand. The zombie howls in pain and tries to shake it off but the snake won't let go.

The other zombies circle around, watching as their comrade flails and thrashes about with the snake still attached to his hand. One of them grabs a stick and tries to pry it off, but the snake just lashes out again, biting him on the leg.

Finally, one of the zombies gets an idea. He picks up a nearby rock and smashes it down onto the snake's head, killing it instantly. The other zombies cheer as the snake falls limp to the ground.

But as they turn back to their fallen comrade, they see that he too has died from his wounds. The other zombies fall silent, realizing that they are not invincible after all. They stare off into the distance, wondering what other dangers might lie ahead in this new world they've found themselves in.

Zombie Snake.

The snake turns into a zombie.

The group is seen moving toward the zombies.

The snake moves toward the group.

The zombies move toward the group.

The group shoots the zombies.

The snake tries to bite Buck.

Buck shoots the snake.

As the snake's body twitches on the ground, Buck can't help but feel a sense of relief. He had always heard that snakes were dangerous, but he had never imagined one turning into a zombie.

The rest of the group seems to have taken notice of the situation, slowly approaching Buck and the lifeless snake. But they're not the only ones moving towards them. The sound of shuffling feet can be heard coming from beyond the trees.

"Get ready," Buck warns them, bringing his shotgun up to his shoulder.

As the first wave of zombies comes into view, Buck starts firing. One by one, they drop to the ground with a sickening thud. But there are too many of them, and soon they're being overrun.

Buck feels something slithering across his leg and looks down to see another zombie snake making its way towards him. Without hesitation, he fires and takes it out.

The group manages to hold off the zombies long enough for help to arrive, but it's a close call. As they make their escape, Buck can't help but wonder what other horrors await them in this new world overrun by the undead.

As Buck pulled the trigger, the snake's body convulsed in one final spasm before it lay still, its zombified state now truly defeated. But the group knew that this wasn't the end. They had to keep moving, had to keep fighting if they were going to survive.

The zombies closed in on them, their mangled bodies rising up from the ground to attack. Buck turned his gun on them and fired, sending bullets flying through their skulls with deadly precision. The others followed suit, their weapons flashing in the dim light of the abandoned city.

But despite their efforts, the zombies kept coming. There seemed to be no end to them, no limit to their relentless hunger for human flesh. The group was outnumbered and outmatched, their options dwindling with each passing moment.

Then suddenly, a new figure emerged from the shadows. It was a woman, dressed in tattered clothes and wielding a machete with deadly skill. She moved with a grace and ferocity that sent chills up Buck's spine.

Without a word, she joined the group in their fight against the zombies. Together they battled through wave after wave of undead attackers, relying on each other's skills and instincts to stay alive.

Finally, as dawn began to break over the desolate cityscape, they emerged victorious. The last of the zombies lay dead at their feet, and they stood together, breathing heavily and covered in blood and sweat.

For a moment there was silence as they absorbed what they had just survived together. Then the woman spoke. "You guys look like you could use some help," she said, her voice rough but friendly.

As the snake fell lifeless to the ground, Buck's heart raced faster than it ever had before. He had never encountered anything like this in his entire life. The zombie snake was just the latest in a series of bizarre and terrifying events that he had encountered since the world had gone to hell.

Buck looked around at his fellow survivors, a group of hardened individuals who had been through their share of terror and loss. But even they seemed shaken by this latest development. Buck couldn't blame them - there seemed to be no end to the horror that this new world had brought.

Just then, a low growling sound erupted from a nearby alleyway. The group turned as one to face the noise, weapons at the ready. But what emerged from the shadows wasn't what they were expecting.

It was a dog.

The animal looked worse for wear - thin and ragged, with matted fur and a limp in its hind leg. But it appeared to be alive and - was that a glimmer of intelligence in its eyes?

The survivors watched as the dog approached them warily, sniffing at their feet. Buck held out a hand hesitantly, and to his surprise, the dog nuzzled against it, letting out a low whine.

"It's okay, boy," Buck said softly. "We're not gonna hurt you."

The dog looked up at him, eyes full of trust and hope. Buck felt something stir in his chest - something he hadn't felt in months.

For the first time since the world had ended, there was a glimmer of hope. And Buck knew that they had to hold onto it with everything they had.

As Buck put down the now-zombified snake with his trusty gun, he couldn't help but feel a wave of relief wash over him. It was bad enough that they were up against a horde of zombies, but to also have a zombie snake after them was just too much.

The group continued to move forward, their steps heavy with exhaustion and fear. Buck could feel his heart pounding in his chest as he looked around at his companions. Matt was panting heavily, sweat pouring down his face while Sarah had a look of determination etched on hers. They were all in this together, fighting for their lives with every step they took.

As they moved closer to the zombies, the group readied their weapons. Buck held his breath as he took aim and fired, taking down a zombie with each shot. Matt swung his axe with deadly precision while Sarah expertly wielded her machete. They were a force to be reckoned with.

Suddenly, the group heard a rustling sound behind them. Buck spun around just in time to see the zombie snake slithering towards him. Instinctively, he raised his gun and pulled the trigger, blasting the snake's head clean off its body.

Breathing hard, Buck turned back to the group and let out a sigh of relief. "Let's keep moving," he said quietly, and the group pushed forward once again. They knew that there were no guarantees in this new world they found themselves in, but as long as they had each other, they had a fighting chance.

Zombie Campers.

Zombie campers are seen stumbling around their tents.

The group rides up to the camp ground.

The zombies stumble out of their tents.

The group shoots the zombies.

More zombies stumble out of their tents.

The group shoots the zombies.

As the last zombie falls to the ground, its decaying flesh barely able to hold itself upright, the group takes a moment to catch their breath. They had been on the move for weeks now, scavenging what little supplies they could find and trying to stay ahead of the undead horde. But something about this particular campsite had caught their attention - perhaps it was the flicker of a dying fire, or the sound of mumbled moans coming from within.

Whatever it was, they had arrived just in time. The zombies may have been slow and disorganized, but they were still dangerous in large numbers. And as they looked around at the dozens of tents still standing in the campsite, they knew that there was no telling how many more undead lay waiting within.

"We need to clear this place out," said the group's leader, a hardened survivor named Marcus. "We can't risk leaving any of these things alive."

The others nodded in agreement, and slowly began making their way through the rows of tents. Every so often, they would come across another group of zombies - some alone, others huddled together in small clusters - and every time they did, they took them out with ruthless efficiency.

But as they pushed deeper into the heart of the campsite, something began to feel off. The zombies they encountered seemed different somehow - more agitated and aggressive than any they had faced before. And when one of them suddenly lunged forward with unexpected speed, catching Marcus off guard and sinking its teeth into his arm, they knew that they had made a fatal mistake.

"Get...out...now," gasped Marcus, as he struggled

As the group continued to shoot down the zombies, they realized that the campsite was not as deserted as they initially thought. They heard screams coming from a nearby tent and quickly ran over to investigate.

Inside the tent, they found a young couple cowering in fear. The man had been bitten by one of the zombies and was slowly turning into one himself. The woman begged them to help him, but they knew it was too late. They had a difficult decision to make - either put him out of his misery or leave him to turn into a zombie.

The group knew what they had to do. The man's cries of pain were unbearable, and they couldn't just leave him there to suffer. One of the group members aimed their gun towards his head and pulled the trigger. Although it was a tough call, it was better than letting him turn into one of those mindless creatures.

As they finished clearing out the rest of the campsite, they realized that this zombie outbreak was only going to get worse. With more and more people being infected each day, it was only a matter of time before they would have to face an entire horde of zombies.

But for now, they would continue on their journey, fighting off any zombies that crossed their path and searching for a safe place to rest their heads at night.

The sound of gunshots echoed through the campsite as the group frantically fired at the undead. Liz, the group's leader, stood tall in the chaos, her eyes scanning the area for any remaining threats.

As Liz reloaded her handgun, she couldn't help but feel a sense of unease. This wasn't like any other zombie outbreak she had encountered before. The undead seemed more aggressive and their movements more coordinated than usual.

Just as she was about to make a move towards the next cluster of tents, a piercing scream filled the air. Liz turned to see one of her own, a young recruit named Mike, pinned down by a pack of zombies. Without hesitation, Liz sprinted towards him, wielding her knife.

The undead turned their attention to Liz, snarling and growling as they lunged forward. But with a practiced swipe of her blade, Liz expertly sliced through their rotting flesh.

Mike scrambled to his feet, blood dripping from a wound on his arm. "Thanks," he gasped as he pulled out his own weapon.

"We have to keep moving," Liz said as she surveyed the area for any more threats.

Suddenly, something caught her eye. A figure in the distance that appeared to be human. But before Liz could investigate further, another wave of zombies emerged from the tents, hungering for flesh.

With no time to waste, Liz and her group fought off the horde and raced towards the unknown figure in the distance. As they drew closer, they realized that it was another survivor - one who seemed to have valuable information about what was really causing this outbreak.

As the last of the zombies falls to the ground, the group lets out a collective sigh of relief. They had been riding for hours and were beginning to think they would never find a safe place to rest. The camp ground was supposed to be a haven, but as they approached they could see that it had been overrun by the undead.

"Let's set up camp over there," one of the survivors said, pointing to a spot on the edge of the clearing. The others nodded in agreement, grateful for a chance to rest their weary bones.

As they began setting up their tents, they couldn't help but wonder how many more zombies might be lurking in the woods. They tried to push the thought from their minds and focus on the task at hand.

But their peace was short-lived. A rustling in the bushes alerted them to another wave of zombies stumbling out of their tents. The survivors quickly drew their weapons and opened fire, taking out several of the undead before they could do any harm.

They knew they couldn't stay here for long - it was only a matter of time before more zombies showed up. But for now, they would rest and gather their strength for whatever lay ahead.

Sally No Brains.

Zombies shoot the groups horses.

The group shoots the zombies.

A zombie walks up behind Sally May.

Sally May looks at the zombie and says "Please don't eat my brain."

The zombie laughs and says "Girl, blondes don't have brains."

Sally May shoots the zombie and says "Don't be a smart ass."

As Sally May scanned the area for any other zombie threats, she realized how dire their situation was. They were stranded in the middle of nowhere with no mode of transportation and limited supplies. The loss of their horses had left them vulnerable to zombie attacks and they were running low on ammunition.

The group decided to take a short break to assess their options when they heard a faint sound in the distance. It sounded like an engine revving, getting closer by the seconds. Sally May strained her eyes, trying to make out where the sound was coming from.

Suddenly, a truck appeared on the horizon, barreling towards them at full speed. The group scrambled to gather their belongings and prepare for a possible confrontation. As the truck pulled up beside them, a rugged-looking man jumped out of the cab and approached them.

"Need a lift?" he asked gruffly.

Sally May didn't trust him, but they had no other options. The group piled into the back of the truck, keeping their weapons close at hand. As they drove away from the zombie-infested wasteland, Sally May couldn't help but feel relieved that they had found a way out.

But little did she know that their journey was only just beginning. The man driving the truck had his own agenda, and it didn't involve helping them survive the apocalypse. As they drove deeper into unknown territory, Sally May wondered if she would ever see her family again or if this would be her final destination.

As the group continued their journey through the post-apocalyptic wasteland, Sally May couldn't help but feel on edge. She had narrowly escaped a close encounter with a zombie, and the memory of its grotesque appearance and rancid breath haunted her.

The rest of the group tried to keep her spirits up, but it was clear that they were all feeling the weight of the world on their shoulders. Suddenly, in the distance, they spotted a glimmer of hope – a small town that seemed to be untouched by the horrors that had ravaged the rest of the world. The group quickened their pace, desperate for some sort of sanctuary from the dangers that surrounded them.

As they approached the town, however, their hopes were quickly dashed. A group of zombies appeared out of nowhere and started attacking them. The group fought back fiercely, firing bullets at the undead horde. But just as they thought they had gained the upper hand, one of the zombies pulled out a shotgun and aimed it at their horses.

Without hesitation, Sally May fired at the zombie, taking it down with a single shot. The rest of the group immediately rallied around her, returning fire and beating back the remaining zombies.

But as they caught their breath and surveyed the damage, Sally May suddenly felt a chill run down her spine. She turned around to see a lone zombie shuffling towards her with a sinister grin on its face.

"Please don't eat my brain," she pleaded with it.

The zombie laughed in response. "Girl, blondes don't have brains."

Sally May didn't hesitate for a second. Raising her gun, she fired off another shot.

As Sally May surveyed the rest of the group, she couldn't help but feel thankful for their quick reflexes. They had managed to take out the zombies that were targeting their horses, but they were still outnumbered and surrounded. The sound of groaning filled the air as more zombies lurched towards them.

With adrenaline pumping through her veins, Sally May raised her gun and took aim at the nearest zombie. She squeezed the trigger and watched as it fell to the ground, lifeless. Her heart was racing as she quickly reloaded her weapon, readying herself for the next attack.

Suddenly, she felt a chill run down her spine as a zombie crept up behind her. She could feel its cold breath on her neck as it leaned in close to her ear. "Please don't eat my brain," Sally May whispered, hoping that maybe this zombie would somehow be different from the rest.

To her surprise, it laughed at her and made a snide comment about blondes not having brains. Sally May gritted her teeth and spun around, raising her gun once again. "Don't be a smart ass," she growled before pulling the trigger.

As the zombie's body hit the ground, Sally May felt a surge of triumph pulse through her body. She knew that there was no room for sentimentality in this new world order, where the living were constantly at risk of being attacked by the undead.

Taking a deep breath, Sally May turned towards her group and signaled for them to move forward. They had to keep going if they wanted to survive.

As the zombie drops to the ground, Sally May takes a deep breath and looks around. It seemed like there were more of them every day. Her once quiet town had become a wasteland, populated only by the undead and those who were still alive, fighting tooth and nail for survival.

She wasn't sure how long she had been on the run for, or how many people she had lost along the way. All she knew was that she needed to keep moving, to keep fighting, in order to stay alive.

Sally May turned to her companions, a ragtag group of survivors who had banded together in order to survive. They were all that was left of her old life - friends, family, colleagues - all gone now.

"We need to find somewhere safe," Sally May said grimly as she kicked at a rock on the ground. "Somewhere we can hunker down for a while and figure out our next move."

The rest of the group nodded in agreement. They were all tired, hungry, and scared. But they knew that they had to keep going.

As they began to move again, they could hear the groans of the undead behind them. Sally May shuddered as she thought about what would happen if they caught up with her. She knew that she had to stay alert, to always be ready for whatever might come next.

And so they continued on, through deserted streets and empty buildings. They were survivors in a world gone mad, fighting for their lives with every step they took.

Rednecks don't have brains.

Zombies surround the group.

Bubba, Brutus and Cletus start crying.

Brutus: "You're not gonna eat our brains, are you?"

The zombies laugh.

Zombie: "Rednecks don't have brains so you have nothing to worry about."

Buck: " Actually, I'm not worried because I have a gun and I know how to use it unlike my cowardly friends , I'm not scared of you."

Zombie: "Well I guess you're gonna shoot us now, huh?"

The group shoots the zombies.

Buck: "I don't know why you guys like to pussy foot around with these things."

As the last zombie falls to the ground, Buck turns to his friends with a smirk. "See, that's how it's done," he says, patting his gun. Bubba, Brutus and Cletus just stare at him in disbelief. They had never seen anyone kill a zombie like that before.

But Buck wasn't done yet. He walked over to the fallen zombies and started kicking them. "That's what you get for coming after us," he yelled. "You mess with us rednecks and you pay the price."

Bubba couldn't take it anymore. "Buck, that's enough," he said. "They're already dead."

But Buck didn't listen. He pulled out a knife and started carving into one of the zombies. "Hey guys, look at this," he said with a twisted smile. "I'm making zombie jerky!"

Bubba, Brutus and Cletus looked on in horror as Buck continued to mutilate the lifeless bodies. They had always known he was a bit extreme, but this was too much even for them.

Suddenly, they heard a noise behind them. They turned around to see more zombies slowly approaching from the woods.

Buck grinned. "Looks like we have some more guests," he said as he reloaded his gun. "Let's give them a warm welcome."

The sound of the gunshots echoes through the empty streets. The group takes a moment to catch their breath and assess their surroundings. Bodies lay scattered around them, all of them undead. Buck leans against a nearby wall, his gun still pointed towards the now lifeless zombies.

Bubba, Brutus and Cletus watch in fear, unsure of what to do or say. They had never seen so much violence before.

Buck turns to them, a look of disgust on his face. "Ya'll are pathetic," he spits out, "Crying like little babies when we're surrounded by these things."

Bubba steps forward, trying to defend himself and his friends. "But Buck, we've never seen anything like this before," he stammers, "How were we supposed to know what to do?"

Buck scoffs at him and shakes his head. "Pathetic," he mutters again. "I'm done wasting my time with you three." He starts to walk away, leaving them behind.

The others watch as Buck disappears into the distance. They're scared and alone, unsure of how to survive in this new world where the dead roam free.

But despite their fear, something begins to stir inside of them - a feeling of anger and determination. They refuse to let Buck's words define them.

Together, they stand up straight and face the zombie horde once again. This time though, they won't cower in fear. Armed with only their courage and determination, they will fight for their survival - no matter what it takes.

As the last zombie falls to the ground, Buck pumps his fist in the air. He turns around to his friends, who are still crying.

"Come on guys, stop being babies," he says. "We've killed zombies before."

Bubba wipes his tears with the back of his hand. "Yeah, but there's so many of them now."

Cletus sniffs. "It ain't natural."

Buck rolls his eyes. "Well, we gotta keep going. We can't let a bunch of undead losers stop us from reaching our destination."

They nod and follow Buck as he leads the way through the sea of zombies. They've been traveling for days now, following a map that Buck found in an abandoned gas station. According to the map, there's a safe haven up north where survivors have gathered to rebuild society.

But the road has been long and dangerous. They've encountered all sorts of horrors along the way - crazed raiders, mutated creatures, and of course, zombies.

Just as they're about to cross a rickety bridge over a deep ravine, they hear a blood-curdling scream.

Buck draws his gun. "What was that?"

Bubba points to the other side of the bridge. "Over there! I think someone's in trouble!"

Without hesitation, Buck charges across the bridge with Bubba and Cletus close behind him. As they reach the other side, they come face to face with a group of heavily-armed raiders who are in the middle of attacking a small group of survivors.

Buck takes aim and fires, taking out one raider

As the group continued down the deserted road, the stench of rotting flesh lingered in the air. Buck led the way, holding his trusty shotgun close to his chest. Bubba, Brutus and Cletus trailed behind him, their faces pale and their hands shaking. They were at a loss for words after what had just happened.

Suddenly, they heard a soft moaning sound coming from the bushes. Buck's senses went on high alert as he gestured for his friends to keep quiet. He crept forward, shotgun at the ready.

As he peeked through the bushes, he saw a young woman lying on the ground. Her skin was pale and her eyes had rolled back into her head. Buck approached cautiously, wondering if she was one of them.

The woman began to stir and let out a low groan. Buck noticed that her clothing was torn and her body was covered in bruises. It was clear that she had been attacked by something.

Buck could feel his heart racing as he contemplated what to do next. He knew that helping her would put himself and his friends at risk, but he couldn't just leave her there to die.

He knelt down beside her and assessed her injuries. She was badly hurt, but still breathing. He made the decision to carry her with them as they continued down the road.

The woman moaned softly as they made their way through the countryside. Buck could feel his heart breaking for her as she struggled to stay alive. He wondered how many more people like her were out here, alone and helpless against the zombie horde.

As they reached an abandoned gas station, Buck laid

Black Neck.

The group is seen walking down the road.

A black man from the farm a mile down the road walks toward the group.

The group walks toward the man.

Cletus: "What is it?"

Bubba: "That there is one of them black necks."

Brutus: "What are they for?"

Bubba: "I don't know."

Cletus: " I heard they have giant cocks and they steal the redneck women."

Brutus: "Buck has a giant cock, does that mean he's a black neck?"

Sally May: "Okay listen you idiots , Buck does have an incredibly large penis but that is because he is blessed and that mans name is Amos and he lives down the road about a mile, I know his wife."

Buck: " Okay Sally May was right about one thing, I have a humungous penis. As for Amos , he's just a farmer like us and I have a question for you, Bubba, What the hell is a black neck?"

Bubba: "It's a country bumpkin with a dark neck."

Buck: "You're still a racist pile of shit."

Bubba: "No I'm not."

Amos: "Hey guys, can someone tell me what is going on?"

Buck: "Yeah, dead people are eating the living and apparently Bubba, Brutus and Cletus should have been born girls because they cry like girls every time they see a zombie."

Amos: "What do you mean dead people?"

Buck: "Have you seen George Romero's movies like Night of the dead, Dawn of the dead and Day of the dead?"

Amos: "Yeah."

Buck: "Well that's what's going on."

Amos: "Holy shit, you mean actual dead people are coming back to life and eating people?"

Buck: "Yeah."

Amos: "I guess that explains why all of those people were biting my wife."

Buck: "Your wife is a zombie?"

Amos: "I don't know, I got out of there before they decided to try to eat me too."

Buck: "Did you get bit?"

Amos: "I don't think so."

A female zombie walks up behind Amos and bites his neck.

Buck shoots the zombie and Amos and says "I guess that was his wife."

Bubba: "I hope I get bit too."

Cletus: "Me too, I hope I get a horomones shot from a zombie woman."

Bubba: "Shut up."

Brutus: "So what now?"

Amos: "Now we barricade the living room of my farmhouse and we try to survive until help comes."

Buck: "How far away is help?"

Amos: "It should have been there by now but I don't think help is coming."

Cut to military base - Interior, General is trying to talk over the chaos of the satellite news head's background noise.

Satellite News Head Guy (Satellite News): "Sir we have no idea what is going on out there, cities are being overrun by the dead and they are eating people alive all because of a blue gas, an extremely poisonous gas that kills instantly when it gets in your lungs, In Los Angeles thousands of people are starting to die as we speak and other parts of the world are experiencing the same problem, reports have already been coming in about Africa and that means that the disease broke out in West Africa which means that it could be anywhere and that means that there might be outbreaks all around the world."

General (Interrupting Satellite News): "So why aren't we stopping it?"

Satellite News Head Guy: "We can't general, our satellites can only traverse the earth if we point them at a general location."

Amos: "Bamberry pie."

Buck: "Okay, let's talk later about my other question, right now we have bigger problems."

Amos: "You mean my wife turning into a zombie?"

Buck: "No, unless I had a horde that was trying to kill me, I would have fucked you wife to death. My wife is dead and not coming back but yours is still kicking."

Amos: "Oops. Who in the hell wants to see a 50 something year old man fucking his young zombie wife? Supposedly she was 26 before she died since she was bitten by a zombie."

Buck: "I would but I don't want my dick bit off. Can't you fuck her when your dead or something?"

Amos: "Shit, I don't know; do zombies come back to life after they die? But if I find out once I die that my wife has decided to eat me like her husband then I might come back as a zombie just so I can fuck her every day for eternity when she dies again."

Brutus: "So how are we supposed to kill a country bumpkin with a dark neck called Amos?"

Cletus: "With our guns and rocket launchers, which I think we should use on him even though he didn't bite me or assault me or make fun of my weight or my dining habits but in fact he picked up all

Bubba: "See that, Amos talked to a girl and now she's dead."

The group leaves and walks off down the road.

The screen turns black.

A barn is seen in the middle of a field inside a fenced enclosure is seen.

A 9 year old boy is seen scooting around in the barren barn.

The boy looks at the ground and sees a candybar on the ground.

He picks it up and sees the words Aug 25th on it with a logo from 2009 on it.

The boy then hears moans from outside.

He goes to a fence post as two zombies walk past the fence into the barn.

The boy goes behind a stack of hay as he watches the zombies walk toward him.

The zombies start looking inside hay stacks but do not find anything.

One of the zombies look under the stack of hay that the boy is hiding behind.

The zombie still does not see him so he walks away back into the sunlight outside of the barn. The other zombie follows suit.

The boy comes out from behind his hiding spot and picks up his candybar while walking out of the barn to greet his father who is standing by a tractor by another fence which opens up into an open pasture.

Two other men are sitting in lawn chairs next to their girlfriends attached by chains to logs instead of doghouse paddles. The women are working with cross-stitches while waiting for their boyfriends return from chasing zombies in Greene County Forrest on probation or who are banned from certain Houston bars because they got too rowdy at night or who have

The black guy dies.

Amos: "Umm guys, I think I'm dying."

Buck: "Why?"

Amos: "Well I don't know but my vision is blurring and my skin feels hot."

Cletus: "You don't think he has the zombie sickness do you?"

Buck: "No he can just be dying from the bite."

The farmhouse lights up as two more zombies walk outside to see what is going on.

Asa: "Damn, we need to get in there."

Sally May: "I don't like this one bit, I get it, you want to save the world by killing all those things but that doesn't change that I have had a long day and I would prefer to go home, have a drink and then come back for another battle tomorrow morning."

Asa: "Sally May one of those things bit your husband, you have to help us."

Sally May "He wasn't my husband anymore, he was dead. Do you understand? He was dead! Dead! Dead! They drove over his body with a pickup truck over, and over and over again just to make sure he was dead because he was a zombie then someone had to blow his head off with a gun because he was still walking around despite being decapitated and now he is going to turn into one of them or worse still come back as one of

Rapping Rednecks.

Bubba: "I'm bored. What are we gonna do?"

Buck: "I've got an idea. Lets shoot zombies and make up rap songs about it."

Bubba: "Okay."

A female zombie walks out into the road.

Buck shoots the zombie and says " That zombie was so ugly she reminds me of your mom. I can't believe you took her to your prom."

Bubba shoots a zombie and says "That one reminds me of my dad, he bought me the best pussy I ever had."

Brutus shoots a zombie and says "Bubba , you're my brother and I love ya and that's why I got to tell the truth. I found proof under your bed that the pussy dad bought you and the best you ever had as sad as it may seem, it was plastic."

Cletus shoots a zombie and says "That's sad your dad had to buy you some but what's even sadder is the fact that the only thing would give it up to you was fake that must just make you want to take your dick and stick it in a light socket."

Sally May shoots a zombie and says "I'm having more fun than that time my brother brought home that whore that turned out to be a nun or that time my dad brought home a barrel of dead monkies or that time my family sang a Christmas carol to a herd of sheep knee deep in snow I don't know what I just said but I'm having fun shooting dead people in the head."

Buck shoots a zombie and says " Everywhere I turn I see dead people. When will they ever learn not to come near me or they'll clearly get shot? They eat your brain. They feel no pain. They got everybody going insane but, what can you do when everything that you thought you knew turns out shit? You can get a gun and fight or run away even though I chose to stay I still hope that they won't try to eat me or try to treat me like a piece of meat because I'll continue to cheat death until I don't have a breath left."

Zombies are seen dancing to Bucks rap.

Everyone starts singing even Buck and the zombies.

Buck: "That was pretty good wasn't it?"

Zombies: "Yes."

Bubba: "Are you sure we can trust these guys?"

Cletus: "Yes I am positive we have an alliance with them now. They would not lie to us they are just really backwards. It's like talking to some Mexicans. All they talk about is drugs, gang banging, and eating shit that crosses their path when they do drugs. These zombies or whatever they are, eat anything that crosses their path. They do drugs for sure."

"Extended Version"

Buck: " You were saying?"

Kenny shoots a zombie and says " I ate some rotten meat this morning. Headed out the door and they're back at it eat they're tainted flesh. I'm staying out my house. The dead are showing their face and I can avoid them I just have to stay inside as long as they don't smell like bacon I'll be good and fine because as long as zombies smell like bacon they won't kill people will they? No. So you die. End of story. Next."

Sharon: "My life sucks because my husband left me for another woman. My love was taken from me. That was a long time ago but it still hurts like it had just happened last night or something when really that was about six to eight months ago. It only brings back bad memories that I wish wouldn't come back so much because then I would have a better life than working at some trailer park and live in some shithole of house with seven kids to take care of by myself. All thanks to Kenny leaving her for another woman when he found out she was also a lesbian which he knew she was before so he shouldn't have left her for her lover should he? Man, I don't know. Sometimes love sucks, you know? You fall in love with something or someone and then it turns your world upside down which happens to be what happened to Kenny and me since he got married to that Betty bitch who is probably getting tail right now

Book ends with Buck shooting them all and walking away.

Title: Zombies Ain't Got No Rhythm

Buck: "So where you from?"

Cletus: "Arkansas."

Buck: "Well wherever you are from as long as you are here at my tuna fish and iced tea party I will fuckin' love you more than that whore I got to sing that carol to. You feel me?"

Cletus: "Whoa whoa, hold up, I aint gay but even I know what you said is fucked up."

Buck: "I aint talkin' to no faggot so either show me how you can cook some fat ass steaks or take your ass down the road."

Cletus: "I thought we had something special but you just proved once and for all you ain't nothin' but a queer."

Buck: "Whatever dude, now get out of my house with those sequins on your pants so bright every time I look at ya I see the mother fuckin' sun."

Cletus: "Fine see if I ever invite you over anymore...I mean even though its not my job or none of my business or I don't care but am I the only one wondering why Bubba has been showering with his clothes on for like three days straight?"

C.W.: "That Buck is some crazy bastard, thinking he can beat death. Letting that gun of his do all the talking

Zombie Dogs.

The group continues walking down the road.

A pack of zombie dogs are seen stalking the group.

The group see the dogs and start running.

The dogs chase the group.

The group chase the dogs.

The dogs attack the group.

The group shoots the dogs.

As the last zombie dog falls to the ground with a whimper, the group catches their breath and looks around. They're in the middle of nowhere, with no sign of civilization in sight. The only sound is the rustling of leaves in the breeze.

"Jesus Christ," says Jack, his hands shaking. "Those things were vicious."

"We can't stay here," says Sarah, looking around nervously. "The noise will attract more of them."

"Agreed," says Simon, the leader of the group. "Let's keep moving. We need to find somewhere safe to regroup."

The group sets off down the road once more, their eyes darting back and forth as they scan their surroundings for any sign of danger. It's not long before they come across a small cabin nestled amongst the trees.

"Perfect," says Simon, a small smile crossing his face. "Everyone be on high alert. We don't know what could be inside."

The group approaches cautiously, their weapons drawn and ready for anything. As they enter the cabin, they see that it's empty - but it's clear that someone was living here recently.

"Looks like whoever was here left in a hurry," says Sarah, examining a pile of dirty dishes in the sink.

Suddenly, they hear a noise outside - a low growling sound that sends chills down their spines.

"Get ready," whispers Simon. "We're not alone."

As the last of the zombie dogs fell to the ground, the group panted heavily, their adrenaline still pumping through their veins. They knew they couldn't stay in one place for long, as any noise or scent might attract more of the undead creatures.

As they continued down the road, they came across a small abandoned convenience store. The windows were boarded up, but the door was slightly ajar.

"Looks like our luck's turned around," one of them said cautiously.

The group entered the store and started scavenging for supplies. They found some canned food and bottled water, but what caught their attention the most was a pile of clothes in the corner.

A young woman in the group picked up a black leather jacket and tried it on.

"Hey, this is so cool! Looks like something out of a movie!" she exclaimed.

One of the guys smirked. "Yeah, you're gonna need all the protection you can get in this world."

Suddenly, they heard a loud banging on the door.

"Shit, we need to move," someone whispered urgently.

They quickly grabbed what they could carry and headed back outside. But as soon as they stepped out into the sunlight, they were greeted by a group of armed men.

"Who are you?" one of them demanded.

"We're just survivors looking for a safe place," one of them answered nervously.

The armed men exchanged glances before lowering their weapons slightly.

"Follow us," one of them said gruffly. "We might be able to help you out."

As the last of the zombie dogs fell to the ground, the group members caught their breaths and looked around. They had been running for what felt like hours and their adrenaline was still pumping through their veins.

One of the members, a tall woman with wild curly hair, turned to her companion and spoke in a hushed voice, "Keep your eyes peeled. There might be more of them around."

The man nodded in agreement and checked his gun. He was a skilled marksman and had already proven his worth during previous encounters with the undead.

The rest of the group followed their lead and moved cautiously forward, scanning their surroundings for any signs of danger. They were a ragtag bunch - survivors from different walks of life thrown together by fate - but they had learned to trust each other over time.

Suddenly, they heard a rustling in the nearby bushes. They immediately tensed up, ready for another attack. But to their surprise, out stepped a lone figure - a young woman with matted hair and tattered clothing.

She looked like she had been wandering for days without food or water. The group hesitated, unsure whether to trust her or not.

But one of them stepped forward, extending a hand in friendship. "Come with us," he said. "We'll keep you safe."

And so the group continued down the road, bonded by their shared struggle to survive in a world overrun by zombies. Their journey was far from over, but they knew that together, they could face whatever lay ahead.

As the group catches their breath, they realize that the zombie dogs weren't the only threat around. Their footsteps had carried them into a deserted town, where the streets were littered with abandoned cars and broken windows. The air was thick with an ominous silence, and it sent shivers down the spines of the group's members.

Suddenly, they heard a faint growling noise coming from one of the houses. The group tensed up and prepared to defend themselves against whatever creature was lurking inside. They cautiously approached the house, guns at the ready.

As they kicked open the door, they found themselves face to face with a horde of zombie rats. The creatures were covered in matted fur and dripping with blood, their glassy eyes fixed on the human intruders.

Without a moment's hesitation, one member of the group raised their rifle and fired a warning shot. The rats scurried away in every direction, but their leader stood his ground.

The remaining members of the group quickly circled around the rat king. They knew that if they didn't take him out, the other rats would just keep coming back.

They charged forward and swung their weapons at the rat king, but he was quick and nimble. He jumped and dodged their attacks with ease, taunting them all the while with his high-pitched squeaks.

Just when it looked like things couldn't get any worse, a new swarm of zombies emerged from the shadows. These ones were even more dangerous than before – they had mutated into giant centipedes.

The group fought for their lives against the new threat and eventually killed them all, but not before sustaining severe injuries.

Fat Zombies.

The group continues walking.

A group of fat zombies walk out of the woods in front of the group.

Buck: "That's sad. It's bad enough that they are dead and ugly but they are also fat."

Fat Zombie: "You have a smart mouth and someone needs to shut you up and as soon as I find someone for the job I'll let you know."

The group shoots the zombies.

Buck: "I don't think you will ever find anyone for that job."

Fat Zombie: "Why you little!"

Part of his face falls out and starts eating the flesh.

Buck: "I don't care what Max said shoot him and keep walking. He is ruining our chances of getting a good meal. Emptying the clip on him is worth more than eating him."

They kill and eat the zombie.

"You still think I need to shut up?" Bucky asks while munching on some fat zombie parts.

"No, you were right when you said he was fat but also slow otherwise I would have shot him more than once." Ziggy said looking at Buck for admiration.

The group continues walking and fighting zombies along the way. They eventually reach a farm house that looks like it has been looted of supplies already since it is empty except for a dead body in the corner called their name for a few minutes then rustle into the ground an undead part Sinestro known as Milton hops out from behind a dresser waiting for them to notice him as if he had just missed them completely from where they came.

Buck: "Oh well isn't this just peachy? I was wondering where you were not to mention how come you look so old or how did you manage to get your arm cut off without making a sound or anyone noticing me here at all? So glad you got my attention since nobody else I hang out with is capable of it maybe this will teach me not to leave my spot at the Inn ever again. Not only that but why would you even care about me

Catle: "I don't think he cares."

Fat Zombie: "You sure are a smartass. How about a fat zombie to the face?"

Buck fires at the fat zombie. He misses and hits the other. They both fall over.

Buck: "Looks like someone beat me to the punch. Excuse me, I think I am going to be sick. I'll be right back." Buck vomits on the ground and passes out.

Bart: "I think this might be where we find our man Johnny Walker Blues."

The group walks to the house and knocks on the door.

A man opens the door and steps outside to look around then comes back inside and closes the door.

Catle shoots his head blowing it off his shoulders. The man falls down and lays on his face not moving or feeling anything anymore ever again. For good!

Insert

Copy

Fat Zombie: "Now that you mention it I might give you a shot. You like making comments to my weight issue don't you?"

Buck: "It is kind of hard not to when you are clearly the fattest zombie I have seen to date."

Fat Zombie: "I ain't done with you yet either. You remember that!"

Buck: "I think I will keep your name in mind and try really hard to remember it so that one day when we meet again we can do lunch!"

They walk off. A giant pig comes out of the forest by Treefeathers.

Giant Pig: "I know what you guys are doing out here and I am tired of seeing it. The farm is under my control now and if one more of you guys walk by I swear I am going to shoot the living crap out of you just like I used to do when there was food here to shoot at! So do yourselves a favor and get off this farm before I kill you all."

The pigs lets them pass after they stop walking. The group continues walking till they reach the destruction field. They stop and look around the site. Each person has a moment alone with their thoughts about what might have happened there but as soon as they collect their thoughts a gunshot goes off somewhere nearby. It sounds almost like someone took a gunshot wound in the arm while standing still by accident but they do not know where it came from because no second gunshot was fired after this first shot rang out so everyone started to calm down.

Giant Mosquitoes .

The group continues walking.

Giant mosquitoes are seen flying toward the group.

The group spray the mosquitoes with bug spray.

The mosquitoes continue coming from every direction.

The group shoots the mosquitoes.

The last mosquito is seen flying toward the group and it's bigger than all the rest.

Buck: "That's the biggest big I've ever seen."

Bubba: "Well, kill it."

Buck: "Shut up stupid." Shoots the mosquito.

As the group continues walking, they come across a clearing where the trees thin out. Suddenly, they hear a loud buzzing noise and look up to see a swarm of giant bees headed their way.

The group frantically sprays themselves with bug spray, hoping it will be enough to keep the bees away. But as the swarm gets closer, it becomes clear that they are not deterred by the spray.

One by one, the group members start to get stung by the bees. Their shrieks of pain echo through the clearing as they try to swat the bees away. But no matter how many they kill, there always seem to be more.

Just when they think all is lost, a man appears from the trees. He's wearing a thick beekeeper suit and carrying a large smoker.

"Get over here!" he yells, gesturing for the group to follow him.

With no other options, they run towards him and he leads them towards a large wooden structure in the middle of the clearing.

"Get inside!" he yells, as he opens the door to reveal a large room filled with shelves of honeycombs.

As they run inside, they can hear the bees buzzing outside, trying to find a way in. But the man starts working his smoker and soon the buzzing fades away.

The group is safe for now, but they have no idea what dangers may lay ahead on their journey through this strange land.

As the mosquito falls to the ground, the group heaves a collective sigh of relief. But their respite is short-lived as they hear a low growl emanating from the trees. Suddenly, a giant bear charges out at them. They all immediately reach for their weapons and start shooting at it. However, the bullets just seem to bounce off its fur, making it even angrier.

The group quickly realizes they need a different approach. Joe pipes up. "I heard that bears don't like loud noises. Maybe we can scare it off with a horn or something?"

Nodding in agreement, they rummage through their belongings until they find a small air horn. One of them blows it as hard as they can, and the sound echoes through the forest. The bear stops in its tracks, momentarily stunned by the noise.

Taking advantage of this moment of confusion, Buck tosses a stick of dynamite in its direction. The explosion startles the bear further and sends it running back into the forest.

Feeling relieved but also shaken from the encounter, the group decides to set up camp for the night and get some rest before continuing their journey. As they lay in their tents, they can hear the faint sounds of rustling in the bushes around them and realize that danger lurks around every corner in this wild land.

As the group continued walking, they left behind the swarm of giant mosquitoes. But despite the calming scenery, Buck couldn't shake off the anxiety feeling that something was off. He had never seen mosquitoes that big, and the last one they encountered sent chills down his spine. The group's relief was short-lived as they heard buzzing again, but this time, it wasn't from mosquitoes.

Suddenly, a loud rumble echoed in the distance, making the ground shake beneath their feet. The group halted their tracks and turned around to see what was causing the commotion. To their surprise, a massive creature emerged from behind the trees, towering over them like a monstrous statue.

The creature was unlike anything Buck had ever seen before. It had a body resembling that of an enormous mosquito, with its massive wings flapping loudly as it flew towards them. Its head was grotesque, with multiple rows of sharp teeth protruding from its gaping maw. Its eyes glowed a menacing green color, pulsating rhythmically like some sort of twisted heartbeat.

The group stood frozen in fear as the ginormous mosquito landed in front of them with a thud, causing tremors that echoed through their bones. They knew they were in for a fight for their lives.

Buck raised his gun and aimed at the creature's head, but before he could pull the trigger, the monster let out an ear-piercing screech that made Buck drop his weapon to cover his ears. The creature lunged forward, grabbing Buck by his arm and lifting him into the air with ease.

Bubba tried to shoot at it to no avail as it swiftly dodged his bullets.

As the group continues to walk, they are suddenly surrounded by an eerie silence. The woods around them had become thicker and darker, and there was an ominous feeling in the air. Suddenly, a strange buzzing sound echoed through the trees, followed by the sound of wings flapping.

The group exchanged glances as they prepared themselves for what was coming. Then, out of nowhere, a swarm of giant mosquitoes descended upon them, their sharp proboscises gleaming in the dark.

Despite their efforts to ward off the ferocious insects with bug spray and gunfire, the mosquitoes kept coming relentlessly. The group fought fiercely, but the mosquitoes seemed to be multiplying rapidly and getting bigger with each passing moment.

Just when it seemed like they were about to be overwhelmed, a deafening crack echoed through the woods as an enormous mosquito appeared from out of nowhere.

The creature was the size of a buffalo and had a wingspan that rivaled that of a small airplane. Its razor-sharp proboscis dripped with venomous saliva, and its eyes glowed with a menacing red hue.

Buck gasped in awe at the sight of it. "That's not just any mosquito," he whispered. "That's a queen mosquito. We'll never survive against her."

Bubba laughed nervously. "Well, Buck, you always have been a drama queen." But his laughter soon turned to terror as the queen mosquito swooped down towards them with lightning speed.

The group scattered in all directions as the monstrous insect began spraying them with highly corrosive venom from its proboscis. Despite their best efforts to evade its attacks, one member after another fell prey to the insects.

Bear Attack.

The group is seen walking down a trail on national park property.

A couple is seen walking about 200 yards in front of the group.

A bear attacks the couple.

Buck shoots the bear.

Another bear attacks Buck.

Buck kicks the bear in the testicles.

The bear is seen rolling on the ground holding its testicles and crying.

Buck: "That should teach you not to attack people."

As Buck stood over the incapacitated bear, he couldn't help but feel a sense of satisfaction. He had always been a bit of a lone wolf, preferring to spend his time in the woods rather than with people. But when he saw that couple being attacked by the bear, something inside him snapped into action.

The adrenaline was still pumping through his veins as he turned back to the group. They were all staring at him with a mixture of fear and admiration. Buck could tell they were all thinking the same thing: this guy is a badass.

But as he looked at them, something else caught his eye. There was a woman in the group who was looking at him with a different kind of admiration. Her name was Rachel, and she had been on his mind since the moment he first saw her.

Buck had always been a bit of a loner, but there was something about Rachel that made him want to open up. He walked over to her and placed a hand on her shoulder.

"Are you alright?" he asked.

She nodded, still looking at him with those big, beautiful eyes. Buck felt himself getting lost in them, and before he knew it, he had leaned in to kiss her.

It was like nothing he had ever experienced before. The softness of her lips, the way she melted into his embrace... Buck knew he was falling for her, hard.

But just as quickly as it started, it was over. They pulled away from each other, both breathing heavily.

"I don't know what's going on here," Rachel said, "but I'm definitely interested in finding out more."

The group watched in awe as Buck took down the second bear with a swift kick to its most sensitive area. The bear whimpered, rolling on its back, and retreated into the woods. Buck walked over to the couple, checking their injuries.

"We need to get you two medical attention," Buck said calmly.

The couple nodded, still in shock from the attack. The group quickly gathered their gear and made their way back down the trail towards the ranger station. As they walked, Buck couldn't help but reflect on how lucky they had been. Two bear attacks in one day could have ended much worse.

When they finally reached the ranger station, they were quickly directed to the medical center on site. The couple was treated for their injuries, while Buck and the rest of the group gave their statements to the rangers.

As they left the park that day, Buck couldn't shake the feeling of adrenaline still coursing through his veins. He knew he had saved those people's lives, but he also knew how easily things could have gone wrong. He made a note to himself to always be prepared for anything when out in nature.

But for now, he was just glad that everyone was safe and that he had been able to use his martial arts skills in such a unique way. Who knew that kicking a bear in the testicles would be so effective?

The group stood in shock as they watched Buck's bravery unfold before their very eyes. They had all heard stories of encounters with grizzly bears, but none of them had ever seen someone fight one off like Buck just did.

As they approached the scene, Buck turned to face them with a look of stern determination. "Everyone stay back," he warned them. "There might be more around here."

The couple who had been attacked were still in shock, but were able to thank Buck for saving their lives. They shared their story with the group, about how they had wandered too far from the trail and ended up surprising the bear and her cubs.

Buck listened intently, sizing up the situation in his head. He knew that if there were cubs around, there was likely to be another bear nearby, and possibly more dangerous than the first.

Suddenly, they heard rustling in some bushes nearby. Buck instinctively reached for his gun, but before he could aim it, another hulking grizzly appeared from between the trees.

This time, however, Buck was ready. Without hesitating, he charged towards the bear and aimed a swift kick between its legs.

The bear let out a deafening roar and fell to the ground writhing in agony. The group watched in disbelief as Buck stood over the bear triumphantly.

"That should teach you not to mess with us," Buck declared as he walked back towards them.

From that day forward, no one ever doubted Buck's strength or bravery again. He had single handedly taken down not one but two grizzlies in a matter of minutes – something that would be talked about for decades.

As the group continued walking down the trail, Buck couldn't help but feel his heart pounding from the adrenaline rush caused by the bear attack. However, he knew that he needed to remain alert, as the forest was full of unpredictable dangers.

Suddenly, Buck heard a rustling noise coming from behind him. He quickly turned around and saw another bear charging towards him with its claws outstretched.

Without hesitation, Buck raised his gun and took aim at the beast. Unfortunately, he realized that he had fired his last bullet when he shot the first bear.

Feeling a sudden surge of fear, Buck knew that he had to think fast. In a split second decision, he decided to use his bare hands to defend himself.

As the bear approached him, Buck remembered the technique his father had taught him as a child. With a swift movement, he lunged forward and delivered a powerful kick to the bear's testicles.

The bear immediately fell to the ground writhing in pain. Buck stood over it, panting heavily as he tried to catch his breath.

"That should teach you not to attack people," he said triumphantly.

Feeling a sense of relief washing over him, Buck knew that he had made it out alive thanks to his quick thinking and bravery. As the rest of the group caught up to him, they congratulated him on his victory and continued down the trail, knowing that they would have to be extra careful from then on.

Naked People.

The group is seen walking in the national park.

10 naked people run by the group.

Buck: "Why are there naked people out here?"

Sally May: "I don't know."

20 more naked people run by the group.

Buck: "What is this, a nudist colony?"

Sally May: "I hope not."

30 more naked people run by the group followed by hundreds of zombies.

Buck: "That makes sense why they are running but I still don't understand why they are naked."

The group run by all the naked people.

As the group continued running, they soon realized that they were being chased by the undead. Sally May had heard about this happening in other national parks, but never imagined that it would happen to her and her group. They ran as fast as they could, trying to put distance between themselves and the zombies.

Amidst the chaos and commotion of the chase, Buck's mind kept wandering back to the naked people they had encountered earlier. He couldn't figure out why they were running around in the buff. Were they part of some sort of cult or was it just a coincidence? The thought of it all was making him feel dizzy and disorientated.

As the group ran past a ranger station, they heard a voice through a megaphone instructing them to come inside. They quickly obliged, slamming the door behind them as dozens of zombies pounded on it from the outside.

Inside, they found a small group of people who had barricaded themselves in the building. But what was most surprising was the fact that they were all naked too. Buck was dumbfounded. It seemed like there were nudists everywhere these days.

Sally May quickly caught on to what was happening. "I think I know what's going on," she said to Buck. "The virus is spreading so quickly that people don't even have time to put clothes on."

Buck didn't know whether to laugh or cry at the absurdity of it all. Naked people running from zombies – what kind of world had they stumbled into?

As they waited for rescue, he couldn't help but notice how attractive some of the women in the room were, their bare bodies glistening in the sun.

As the group ran with all the naked people, they could hear the growls and moans of the zombies getting closer. Buck couldn't help but wonder why so many people would be at a nudist colony in the middle of a national park. Sally May was equally puzzled but there was no time to waste on questions.

They all ran towards a nearby cabin hoping to find shelter from the impending doom that was fast approaching. As they approached the cabin, they noticed a group of people frantically trying to board up the windows and doors.

"Quickly, help us!" one of the people shouted as they ran towards the group.

Without hesitation, Buck and Sally May helped them with the boards, working together to secure the cabin. The naked people who had been running with them joined in, and soon they were all working together like a well-oiled machine.

Just as they finished securing one of the windows, a zombie smashed through another window and made its way into the cabin. The group fought off the zombie with whatever they could find - wooden planks, kitchen utensils, even their bare hands.

As they battled the zombie, Buck couldn't help but notice one of the naked women beside him. She was covered in sweat and dirt, but still managed to look breathtakingly beautiful. He was lost in his thoughts when Sally May's scream brought him back to reality.

Another zombie had snuck up behind Sally May, grabbing her by her hair. Buck immediately ran towards her and pulled her away from the zombie's grasp. They fought off the zombie together, their bodies pressed close against each other as they struggled to defeat their common enemy.

As the group ran by the naked people, Sally May couldn't help but feel a strange sensation in her stomach. It wasn't fear or disgust, as one might expect, but rather a sudden urge to join in the revelry. She looked over at Buck but he was too focused on the zombies to notice her inner turmoil.

Suddenly, one of the naked people slowed down and turned to face Sally May. His skin was sun-kissed and his eyes sparkled mischievously in the sunlight. Before she could even register what was happening, he grabbed her hand and pulled her into the center of the group.

Sally May felt a rush of excitement course through her body as she shed her clothing and joined in their wild dance. The sound of pounding drums and howling screams filled her ears as she let herself be swept up in their primal ritual.

But just as suddenly as it had started, the group dispersed and Sally May found herself standing alone amidst the chaos. She looked around for Buck but he was nowhere to be found.

Feeling vulnerable and exposed, Sally May quickly put on her clothes and set off in search of her companions. As she walked, she couldn't shake the feeling that something inside her had changed forever.

As they ran, Buck couldn't help but notice the sun-kissed skin of the naked people bouncing in the wind. For some reason, it excited him. Maybe it was the adrenaline rush of running for their lives, or maybe it was the thrill of seeing so many naked bodies all at once. Either way, he couldn't deny how turned on he was.

Sally May seemed to be feeling a similar way. Despite the chaos around them, she couldn't help but glance over at Buck every once in a while, her eyes full of desire.

As they approached a clearing, they saw a cabin up ahead. Without hesitation, they dashed inside and locked the door behind them. It wasn't until then that Buck turned to Sally May and suddenly grabbed her by the waist.

"What are you doing?!" she exclaimed, but she didn't push him away.

"I don't know," Buck replied, his voice breathless. "I just can't help myself."

Sally May's eyes widened as Buck leaned in and kissed her deeply. She melted into his arms, their bodies pressed together with an intensity that neither of them could explain.

As they pulled away from each other, panting heavily, they realized that they had forgotten about the zombies outside. But at that moment, they didn't care. For now, all that mattered was their own physical desires, and nothing else.

Zombie Cops.

The group runs out of the national park and stops on the road to catch their breath.

Zombie cops surround the group with gun in hand.

Zombie Cop: "Don't move."

The group move out of the way and the zombies shoot each other.

Buck: "Talk about dumb cops."

As the group catches their breath, they take a moment to survey their surroundings. They are on a road that winds through the trees, with no civilization in sight. The only sound is the rustle of leaves in the wind.

Suddenly, they hear the clicking of boots on pavement. They turn to see a group of zombie cops approaching them, guns drawn. The group freezes in fear, unsure of what to do.

But then something strange happens: the zombie cops turn on each other, their trigger fingers twitching uncontrollably. Blood splatters across the road as their bullets find unintended targets.

The group looks at each other in stunned silence before Buck breaks it with a sarcastic quip. But as they try to move away from the carnage, they realize something even more terrifying: they are not alone.

A horde of zombies emerges from the trees, attracted by the sound of gunfire. The group starts to run, but they know it's only a matter of time before they're overtaken.

Desperate for shelter, they spot an abandoned cabin up ahead and make a break for it. But as they barricade themselves inside, they realize that they've only traded one danger for another.

When the sun sets and darkness falls over the forest, they hear whispers and creaks outside. It seems as though someone or something is watching them from beyond the door.

As tense hours pass, the group realizes that their fight for survival has only just begun. And with each passing moment, it becomes clearer that their chances of making it out alive are slim at best.

As the group moved out of the way, they couldn't believe their luck. The zombie cops, it seemed, were so disoriented that they ended up shooting each other instead of the survivors. Buck's comment echoed through the group, breaking their stunned silence.

But their respite was short-lived. Out of the bush came a pack of feral dogs, eyes glowing and teeth bared. They lunged at the group, snarling and snapping as they went.

Despite their exhaustion from fleeing the zombie-infested park, survival instincts kicked in, and the group fought back with all their might. Jerry grabbed a nearby stick and swung it at the nearest dog with all his strength. With a sickening crunch, it connected with its skull and sent it tumbling to the ground.

Mary scrambled to find anything she could use as a weapon but found nothing useful amidst the chaos. Instead, she followed Buck's lead and used her fists to pummel one of the dogs trying to grab onto her leg.

Finally, after what felt like an eternity of fighting, they managed to fight off the pack of feral dogs. As they caught their breath once again, they realized they were not safe yet.

More zombie cops were closing in on them from behind, all with guns drawn and determined expressions etched onto their undead faces.

As soon as the last zombie cop falls to the ground, the group lets out a collective sigh of relief. They stand there for a moment, bewildered and shocked by what just happened. Buck takes charge and turns to the others.

Buck: "Let's keep moving before more of them show up."

The group nods in agreement and quickly sets off down the road, heads swiveling left and right as they scan for any signs of danger. After several minutes of fast-paced walking, they come across a deserted gas station. They decide to stop and take a breather.

As they walk around the abandoned station, they see that it's been ransacked. Shelves are empty and overturned, glass is shattered everywhere, and blood stains the floor. The group tenses up at the sight of it all.

Suzy: "This is giving me major bad vibes. Maybe we should leave?"

Buck: "No, we need to search this place for supplies. We don't know how long we'll be out here."

The group splits up and starts searching the station for any useful items. Buck checks behind the counter while Suzy looks in the back room. Suddenly, she lets out a scream.

Suzy: "Guys! You need to come see this!"

The rest of the group runs over to where Suzy is standing and sees what was in the back room - a woman tied up with rope and gagged.

Buck: "We need to untie her and get her out of here."

As soon as they untie her, she starts sobbing uncontrollably.

The group quickly realized that these were not ordinary cops, but zombie cops, infected and turned by the virus that had been spreading rapidly through the city. They looked at each other in shock and horror, wondering what other horrors awaited them in this post-apocalyptic wasteland.

As they stood there frozen, a loud growling noise broke the silence. They turned around to see a pack of flesh-eating zombies running towards them. The group quickly drew their weapons and prepared to fight.

Samantha, the group's leader, took charge. "We have to move now! Follow me!" she shouted, as she ran towards the nearby abandoned gas station.

The group followed her lead, firing their weapons at the approaching zombies. They finally reached the gas station and barricaded themselves inside, hoping to find safety in its walls.

But their respite was short-lived. The zombies soon found their way inside the gas station, crashing through windows and doors. The group was caught off guard as they fell back under the ferocious assault.

They were outnumbered and outmatched. But they fought bravely until there was no escape left. With heavy hearts, they made the ultimate sacrifice - sacrificing their own lives for the sake of humanity.

As Samantha breathed her last breaths, she whispered to her companions: "I'm sorry we couldn't make it out of here alive. But promise me you'll keep fighting till your last breaths too. Remember that our legacy lives on in each one of you."

And with those words, Samantha closed her eyes and drew her last breaths - a hero who gave everything she had for a better world.

Psycho Zombie.

The group is seen walking down the road.

A zombie runs out of the woods with an axe and starts swinging it at the group.

The group dodges the axe.

The zombie continues swinging the axe at the group.

Buck catches the axe and hits the zombie in the face with the back of it knocking the zombie to the ground.

The zombie stands up and tries to swing the axe at the group again and accidently cuts his own head off.

Buck: "Now look what you did."

The group continued walking down the winding road, following its curves and dips in the landscape, their conversation light and cheerful. They were in the middle of banter about the best way to cook a steak, when suddenly the sound of twigs snapping and leaves rustling exploded from the woods beside them.

A zombie emerged, wielding an axe in one hand and an air of distraction in the other. He was swaying back and forth, his eyes wild and unfocused, and before any of them could react, he began swinging the axe at the group.

The group jumped out of the way, narrowly avoiding the blade each time it came close. There was a pause as the zombie seemed uncertain of his next move, until he let out a guttural groan and lunged for the axe again, swinging it around in a wide arc.

Acting quickly, Buck snatched the axe from the zombie and, using the back of it, hit him square in the face. The zombie fell back, crashing to the ground like a sack of potatoes.

But the zombie still wasn't finished, and before anyone could blink, he was back on his feet. He made another lunge for the axe, this time with a bit more cunning in his movements, but as he swung it round again, he accidentally sliced his own head off.

Everyone in the group stood stunned, their eyes wide with shock. Buck held the axe in his hands, its blade still dripping with the undead's blood. He looked down at the now decapitated zombie, then up to the group, and said with a hint of a smirk, "Now look what you did."

Zombie Farmers.

Hundreds of zombies are seen on a farm.

The group is seen walking down the road near the farm.

A zombie bites Bubba.

Bubba shoots the zombie.

The zombies move toward the group.

Buck shoots the zombies with an rpg.

Bubba: "Damn it, that son of a bitch bit me."

Buck looked at Bubba's wound and saw the bite marks were deep. It was only a matter of time before Bubba would turn into a zombie. Buck knew what had to be done, but he couldn't bring himself to do it just yet.

The group continued down the road, trying to find a safe haven away from the approaching zombie horde. The sky was getting darker and Buck knew they didn't have much time left. They needed to find shelter fast.

They stumbled upon an old abandoned factory and decided to take refuge inside. As they made their way through the dark and dusty building, they heard whispers coming from a corner of the room. They slowly approached, weapons at the ready, but what they found was unexpected.

A group of survivors, huddled in a small corner of the room, stared back at them in fear. They had been hiding there for days, scared to come out because of the zombies outside.

Buck knew they needed all the help they could get if they were going to make it through this. He convinced the survivors to join forces with them and together they barricaded themselves inside the factory.

As the night went on, the zombies outside grew louder and more persistent. The group worked tirelessly, fortifying their defenses with whatever resources they could find within the factory's walls.

But as dawn approached, Bubba's condition worsened. Buck knew what had to be done and with a heavy heart, he raised his gun and took aim at his friend.

The sound of the shot echoed throughout the factory and for a brief moment, everything was silent. But then the zombies outside began banging on the doors

As they continued down the road, Bubba's wound grew more painful. He could feel the venomous infection creeping through his veins like a fire. He knew what was coming next - he would turn into one of those things. The thought of it made him sick to his stomach.

The group came to a halt as more zombies emerged from the fields. They were surrounded. Bubba could feel his heart racing faster than ever before. He knew that this would be his last stand.

Buck pulled out his rocket launcher and aimed it at the approaching horde. He fired, sending a fiery explosion through the ranks of the undead. The blast was so powerful that Bubba was knocked off his feet.

As he lay there, he felt a strange pull on his consciousness. The infection was taking hold, and he could feel himself slipping away from the world of the living. But then something happened that he did not expect - he began to change.

He felt a new strength coursing through his body, and he rose to his feet once again. But this time, he was not alone. Dozens of other undead creatures stood by his side, ready to take on the living.

And so began the legend of Bubba and his zombie army, who roamed the post-apocalyptic wasteland in search of new victims to add to their ranks. The survivors whispered their name in fear, for they knew that no one could stop them - not even death itself.

The group quickly realized that they were in trouble. The horde of zombies was closing in on them fast, and their only option was to take refuge on the farm nearby. Without a second thought, they rushed toward the farmhouse, hoping to find some shelter.

As they approached the farm, they could see that it had been abandoned for quite some time. The windows were boarded up, and there was no sign of life inside. Nevertheless, they had to try. They opened the door and rushed inside.

The inside of the farmhouse was dark and musty, with cobwebs hanging from the ceiling. There was a heavy silence that hung in the air. Suddenly, a moan broke the silence, followed by another. They realized that they were not alone. There were zombies hiding inside the farmhouse.

The group drew their weapons as the zombies began to emerge from the shadows, their eyes glowing in the darkness. Bubba aimed his gun at one of them and fired, striking it in the head with deadly accuracy. But there were too many of them to take down one by one.

Buck took out his RPG and aimed it at the horde outside. He fired, sending a massive explosion through the air and scattering body parts everywhere. The group breathed a sigh of relief as they watched the zombies outside being blown apart.

As they caught their breath, Bubba let out a cry of pain, grabbing his arm where he had been bitten earlier. The others rushed to his side as he fell to the ground, writhing in agony.

"DAMN IT!" he shouted. "That son of a bitch bit me."

The group quickly assessed Bubba's wound and realized that it was a severe zombie bite. They knew that time was running out for him, and they needed to find shelter soon.

As they continued walking down the road, they stumbled upon an abandoned warehouse. Buck kicked open the door, and the group hurried inside, barricading the entrance with all the heavy objects they could find.

Bubba's condition was deteriorating fast. His skin had turned a sickly pale shade, and his eyes were starting to cloud over. The group knew that he didn't have much time left.

Suddenly, Bubba let out a bloodcurdling scream as he began convulsing on the ground. The others tried to hold him down, but his strength was too much for them.

It was then that they realized that they had no other choice. They had to put Bubba down before he turned into one of them.

As tears streamed down their faces, Buck raised his shotgun and pulled the trigger. The sound echoed through the warehouse as Bubba's lifeless body lay still on the ground.

The group knew that they couldn't stay there forever. They needed to keep moving if they wanted any chance at survival.

But as they stepped outside, they were met with an even greater horror. The entire street was teeming with zombies - more than they had ever seen before.

Their only chance was to fight and make a break for it, hoping to find another safe haven somewhere down the line. And so they charged forward into the swarm, guns blazing, determined to live another day.

Zombie Bubba.

The group continues walking down the road.

Bubba turns into a zombie and bites Brutus.

Brutus: "Ouch."

Buck: "Hey Bubba?"

Bubba: "What?"

Buck: "Can I have your pistol?"

Bubba gives his pistol to Buck.

Buck: "Thanks." Shoots Bubba with his own pistol.

As the group continued their journey, they were all in shock at what had just happened. The sound of the gunshot echoed in the quiet forest.

Brutus began to feel woozy, and his vision started to blur. He knew what was happening. The infection from Bubba's bite was spreading through his veins, and there was no turning back.

Buck looked over at Brutus, who had now fallen to the ground. He knew he had to act fast. He could see the veins in Brutus' neck swelling, and the skin turning a sickly shade of green. Buck raised his pistol and hesitated for a moment before firing.

The shot rang out, and Brutus' body jerked violently before falling limp on the ground. Buck knew he had just killed his friend, but it was better than leaving him as a zombie to harm others.

As Buck sat next to Brutus' lifeless body, he couldn't help but question how much longer they could survive in this world overrun by the undead.

The group looked in horror as Bubba's lifeless body slumped to the ground. They had all known that something like this was bound to happen. The world had gone to hell and each day was a battle for survival.

Brutus, who had been bitten by Bubba, knew what was coming next. He started to feel the fever taking hold of him. He knew that soon he would turn into one of those things.

Buck watched as Brutus started to convulse. His eyes wide with terror, Buck knew there was only one thing he could do to save the group from another potential zombie attack.

Without hesitation, Buck raised the pistol and aimed it at Brutus's forehead. The sound of the gunshot echoed through the deserted street as Brutus's body went limp.

Silence enveloped them as they all stood there, processing what had just happened. They had lost two members in a matter of minutes.

"We can't stay here," said Buck, breaking the silence. "We need to keep moving."

The group nodded in agreement as they continued on down the road, their eyes scanning their surroundings for any more signs of danger. They knew that they couldn't let their guard down again, not even for a second.

Brutus stumbled back from the sudden attack and clutched his bitten arm, feeling weakness creeping in. Buck, quick on his feet, caught him before he could fall over.

"Easy there, Brutus," Buck said, supporting him. "We're gonna get you some help."

Brutus gasped for breath, feeling his heart racing with fear and pain. He knew that being bitten by a zombie would turn him into one of them soon enough. The thought of losing control of his body and becoming a mindless monster was overwhelming.

Buck looked around nervously, scanning the deserted road for any signs of danger. He knew that they couldn't stay out in the open like this for long.

"We gotta find somewhere safe to hole up," he muttered to himself.

Brutus tried to speak, but his throat was tight with fear and pain. He could feel the infection spreading through his bloodstream, making him weaker by the second.

Suddenly, Buck grabbed his arm and pulled him towards an old abandoned warehouse on the outskirts of town.

"Come on," he urged. "We might be able to find some supplies in there."

As they approached the warehouse, Brutus felt a chill run down his spine. Something about the place felt wrong - like they were walking straight into a trap. But he knew that they had no other choice - they had to find shelter before it was too late.

Buck kicked open the door and led Brutus inside. The air was thick with dust and the smell of decay - but it was still better than being out in the open with zombies all around them.

Brutus collapsed onto the ground,

The group stood in shock as the once jovial Bubba turned into a snarling, undead creature. His eyes clouded over with a milky white film, and his skin took on a sickly grey hue. Brutus stumbled back, clutching at his bitten arm in pain.

Buck wasted no time. He knew that if Bubba had turned, there was no hope for him. He needed to be put down before he became a danger to the rest of the group. Without hesitation, Buck asked for Bubba's pistol.

Bubba handed it over willingly, perhaps not even realizing what was happening to him. Buck took aim and fired a single shot, striking Bubba in the forehead. The zombie's body convulsed for a moment before falling lifeless to the ground.

Silence hung heavy in the air as the group stared at Bubba's lifeless form. It was a harsh reminder of just how dangerous their new reality was. They were no longer in a world where laws and order existed; they were in a world where survival meant making tough choices - choices that could mean the difference between life and death.

Brutus let out a pained groan, reminding the group that they needed to keep moving. The road stretched out before them, seemingly endless, but they had to keep going. They had to find safety before it was too late.

Zombie Brutus.

The group continues walking down the road.

Brutus turns into a zombie and bites Cletus.

Cletus: "You son of a bitch."

The group moves off the road as traffic thickens.

Buck: "Brutus?"

Brutus: "Yeah."

Buck: "You dropped your gun in the street."

Brutus walks out into the road to get his gun and is hit by a truck.

Cletus stared in shock as Brutus stumbled backward, a growl escaping from his throat. In a matter of seconds, Brutus transformed into a snarling, flesh-eating zombie.

Cletus backed up, his hand reaching for his gun. But before he could even draw it from its holster, Brutus lunged forward and sank his teeth into Cletus's arm.

Pain shot up Cletus's arm as he struggled to pull away. "You son of a bitch!" he yelled as he finally managed to wrench himself free.

The group quickly moved off the road as traffic began to thicken. They huddled together, unsure of what to do next.

As they tried to come up with a plan, Buck noticed something in the street. "Brutus?" he called out. "You dropped your gun in the street."

Without thinking, Brutus walked out into the road to retrieve his weapon. But just as he reached for it, a truck came barreling down the road and slammed into him, sending him flying.

The group stood frozen in shock as Brutus lay motionless on the pavement. It was over. He was gone.

As the group rushes to Brutus' side, they realize that it's too late. He takes a few last gasps of breath and then goes still. Cletus is still fuming after being bitten, but he can't help feeling a sense of loss for his former friend.

They quickly realize that they need to get off the road and find a safe place to hunker down for the night. They come across an abandoned gas station and decide it's as good a spot as any. They barricade the doors and windows as best they can and settle in for the night.

But their peace is short-lived when they hear a scratching at the door. They know they should leave well enough alone, but curiosity gets the better of them. They slowly open the door to find a young girl huddled on the ground, crying.

She tells them her name is Lily and that she's been on her own since her parents were attacked by zombies. Despite their reservations about taking on another person, they can't bring themselves to leave her alone.

As the days go on, Lily becomes a valuable member of the group. She has a knack for finding food and supplies, and she brings a sense of hope to their otherwise grim situation.

But their newfound family is tested once again when Cletus starts showing signs of turning into a zombie. They all know what needs to be done, but it doesn't make it any easier when Buck has to put him down.

As they mourn yet another loss, they realize that this world has changed them forever. But together, they'll keep fighting for survival, no matter what comes their way.

The group stares in horror as Brutus' body is mangled under the wheels of the truck. Cletus clutches his bitten arm, eyes widening in fear.

Suddenly, Brutus' body twitches and his eyes snap open. His skin is pale and his veins pulse with an eerie glow.

Buck steps back, gun raised. "What the hell? He's still alive?"

Brutus climbs to his feet, swaying slightly. His eyes fix on Cletus, who raises a trembling hand. "Stay back, man."

But Brutus lunges forward, snarling. The group staggers back, unsure how to react as Brutus attacks Cletus with inhuman strength.

Cletus screams, blood spattering across the pavement as Brutus tears at his flesh. The others scramble to pull him off, but he's too strong.

Finally, they manage to subdue him, holding him down as he thrashes and snarls.

"He's infected," one of them says grimly. "He's turned into one of them."

The group looks at each other in despair. They're trapped in a world where anyone can become a zombie at any moment - and there's no way to know who will turn next.

The group stares in shock as Brutus' lifeless body lies in the road. Cletus grabs Buck's arm for support, and they both watch as the truck driver jumps down from the cab and sprints toward them.

"Is he dead?" the driver asks, panting heavily.

"Yeah," Buck replies, voice strained.

"I'm so sorry," the driver says, his eyes filling with tears. "I didn't see him...I was texting."

Cletus lunges at the driver, fury in his eyes. Buck holds him back as the rest of the group surrounds them.

"What the hell is wrong with you?!" Cletus yells at the driver, struggling against Buck's grasp. "You killed him!"

The driver hangs his head in shame, tears streaming down his face. "I know," he says, voice breaking. "I didn't mean to."

The group stands in stunned silence for a few more moments before Cletus finally collapses onto the pavement, overcome with grief. Buck kneels down beside him and puts an arm around his shoulder, trying to comfort him as best he can.

The others stand around awkwardly, not knowing what to say or do.

Finally, one of them begins to speak up. "We have to keep moving," she says softly. "We can't just stay here."

The group nods solemnly and begins to make their way down the road once more, leaving Brutus' body behind as they go. Cletus takes one last look over his shoulder, tears still streaming down his face, before forcing himself to keep up with the others.

Zombie Cletus.

The group continue walking.

Cletus turns into a zombie and grabs what he thinks is Bucks arm and starts biting it.

Zombie: "Hey, stop biting me."

Cletus: "Sorry, I thought you were someone else."

Buck shoots Cletus and the zombie and says "Bite that."

Sally May and Buck walk away.

As Sally May and Buck trudged down the deserted street, they couldn't help but feel uneasy. They had been on the run for days now, hiding from the undead and scavenging what little supplies they could find.

But despite their efforts, it seemed like the world was against them. Cletus's sudden turn into a zombie had only reinforced their growing sense of dread.

Sally May felt a knot of fear twist in her stomach. She had grown close to Buck during their journey, and seeing his coldness towards Cletus had made her realize just how dangerous this world had become.

But as they continued walking, she couldn't shake the feeling that something was watching them. Every creak of a floorboard or rustle of leaves sent shivers down her spine.

Suddenly Buck stopped in his tracks, causing Sally May to bump into him. He quickly spun around, rifle at the ready.

"What is it?" she whispered, heart pounding in her chest.

"I thought I saw movement up ahead," he replied, scanning the area carefully.

Together they crept forward, guns drawn and ready for anything. But as they reached a bend in the road, they saw something that made their blood run cold.

A horde of zombies was shuffling towards them, their grotesque faces twisted in hunger. Sally May's mind went blank with terror as she realized they were surrounded.

But Buck had other ideas. Without hesitation he raised his gun and fired off a shot, the sound echoing through empty streets. The zombies turned towards them, drawn by the noise.

Sally May watched in amazement as Buck fought off wave after wave of undead

As they walked, the sun began to dip below the horizon, spreading a warm glow across the barren wasteland. Sally May shivered and hugged herself, wishing she had brought a jacket on their trip.

Buck noticed her shivering and took off his flannel shirt, offering it to her. "You look cold," he said in a low voice.

Sally May hesitated, but then took the shirt. As she slipped it on, she couldn't help but breathe in Buck's scent – musky and masculine with a hint of sweat. She felt a flush run through her body and couldn't help but wonder what it would be like to be held by him.

Suddenly, they heard a rustling noise behind them. Buck turned around, his gun ready, but all he saw was movement in the bushes.

"Stay here," he told Sally May as he approached the bushes with caution.

As he got closer, a woman appeared from the shadows, holding her hands up in surrender. She was thin and dirty with matted hair and torn clothing.

"Please," she said in a hoarse voice. "I need your help."

Buck lowered his gun and motioned for Sally May to come forward. The woman explained that she had been bitten by one of the zombies and needed medical attention.

Sally May felt a pang of sympathy for the woman and offered to help. As they tended to her wounds, Sally May couldn't help but notice how beautiful the stranger's eyes were – a deep green that seemed to shine even in the dim light.

They decided to travel together – safety in numbers, Buck reasoned. For the rest of the night

As they walked away from the gruesome scene, Sally May couldn't help but feel a sense of unease settling in the pit of her stomach. She knew that it was only a matter of time before they would succumb to the same fate as Cletus if they weren't careful.

Buck sensed her unease and placed a comforting arm around her shoulders. "Don't worry, Sally May," he said, "we'll just have to be extra careful from now on."

Sally May nodded, but she couldn't shake off the feeling of dread that weighed heavily on her. They continued walking in silence for a few more minutes until they stumbled upon an abandoned gas station.

"We should scavenge what we can from here," Buck said, his eyes scanning the area for any signs of danger.

Sally May agreed and started rummaging through the shelves for any supplies they could use. As she was looking, she heard a faint groaning sound coming from outside.

She turned to warn Buck but before she could say anything, he had already drawn his gun and was heading out the door. Sally May followed closely behind him and they found themselves face to face with a group of zombies.

Buck wasted no time in shooting them down one by one while Sally May provided backup with her own weapon. They managed to take down the last zombie just as more began to emerge from nearby buildings.

"We need to get out of here," Buck said, grabbing Sally May's hand and pulling her towards the back exit.

They ran as fast as they could, but Sally May stumbled and fell to the ground, twisting her ankle in the process. Buck helped her walk.

But as they continued walking, Sally May couldn't shake off the unease that settled in her heart. Cletus, who was once a friend, had turned into a zombie right before their eyes. She knew this wasn't the world they knew before, but it still felt surreal.

Buck noticed Sally May's unease and gave her a reassuring nod. But even his presence couldn't shake off the chill in the air.

As they continued down the deserted street, they could hear faint groans in the distance. They quickened their pace, hoping to avoid any more unexpected encounters.

But it was too late. As they turned a corner, they were met with a horde of zombies. The groans they heard earlier were getting louder and closer.

Buck raised his gun, ready to fight off the approaching undead. Sally May felt panic grip her heart. They were outnumbered and outmatched.

But as the zombies got closer and closer, something strange happened. One by one, they stopped in their tracks and fell to the ground.

Sally May couldn't believe her eyes as she watched the horde of zombies decrease in number until there were none left standing.

Buck lowered his gun, perplexed by what just happened. And then they saw him- a lone man standing at the end of the street with an unknown device in his hand.

He approached them with caution but extended a friendly hand. "I'm Steve," he said. "And I think I've found a way to stop this virus from spreading."

Survivors.

Traffic thickens as Buck and Sally May are seen getting into a car and driving away.

Driver: "Where to?"

Buck: "Anywhere but here."

Driver: "I heard it's been crazy around here."

Sally May sat silently in the backseat, staring out the window as the driver navigated through the busy city streets. She couldn't shake off the feeling of exhaustion that had been hanging over her ever since she got the news. But she was grateful for Buck, grateful that he was there to hold her hand and help her through it all.

As they crossed the bridge leading out of the city, Buck took a deep breath and turned to face Sally May. "We don't have to keep running," he said gently. "We could go back."

Sally May shook her head, tears welling up in her eyes. "I can't go back there. I can't face them, not after what happened."

Buck nodded understandingly and reached over to grip her hand. "Then we'll keep going," he said firmly. "We'll find a place where we can start over, where nobody knows us."

They drove on in silence for several hours, passing through small towns and winding country roads until they came upon a sign that read "Welcome to Blue Ridge Mountains". Sally May felt a flicker of hope stir inside her; maybe this was where they were meant to be.

As they made their way up into the mountains, Buck pulled off onto a dirt road that wound through a dense forest. Finally, they came upon a clearing overlooking a tranquil valley below. The sun was setting in a blaze of orange and red, casting an ethereal glow over everything.

"This is it," Buck said softly, and Sally May knew that he was right. This was where they would make their new home, far away from their past and whatever lay ahead.

Sally May nodded in agreement, her eyes darting around the congested streets as they made their way through the city. It had been months since she had seen the outside world, trapped inside her small apartment with Buck by her side. But she knew that it was time to leave.

They drove for hours, the landscape passing them by in a blur of green and grey. Sally May felt her pulse quicken as they left the city behind, the air growing fresher with each passing mile. As the sun began to set on the horizon, Buck finally spoke up.

"Pull over here," he said, pointing to a small dirt road that wound its way up into the hills.

The driver did as he was told, and Buck and Sally May got out of the car and started walking up the dusty path. Soon, they came to a clearing overlooking a picturesque valley, and Sally May felt her breath catch in her throat.

"This is beautiful," she whispered.

Buck smiled down at her, his eyes sparkling in the fading light. "I thought you might like it."

As they sat down on a nearby rock, Sally May leaned into Buck's side and breathed in his scent. She knew that they couldn't stay here forever, but for now, it was enough just to be with him.

They stayed there for hours, watching the stars twinkle overhead and listening to the sound of crickets chirping in the bushes. When they finally made their way back down to the car, they were both exhausted but happy.

"Where to now?" asked the driver as they climbed back inside.

Buck grinned at Sally May as he reached for her hand.

Buck nodded, keeping his eyes trained straight ahead. Sally May sat in the passenger seat, staring out the window at the blur of cars streaking by. She could feel the tension radiating off of Buck in waves; it was almost suffocating.

The driver's words hung in the air like a dark cloud. "Crazy" didn't even begin to describe the chaos that had erupted back at their place.

Sally May shuddered as she remembered the shouting, the breaking glass, and Buck's fists clenching at his sides.

"Let's just get out of here," Buck muttered. "I can't take it anymore."

The driver nodded, seemingly understanding their need for escape. He expertly wove through traffic, taking them down side streets and back alleys until they were far away from the madness of their old life.

It wasn't until they were miles away, tucked safely inside a cozy little motel room, that Sally May finally found her voice.

"What do we do now?" she asked, twisting her hands together in her lap. "We can't keep running forever."

Buck sighed heavily, raking a hand through his hair. "I know. But right now...right now we just need to rest. Figure out our next move."

Sally May nodded, curling up against him as they settled into bed. She knew deep down that things were far from over - but for now, she was content to just be with Buck and forget about the chaos they had left behind.

Sally May let out a heavy sigh as they drove past the busy streets, the city lights twinkling in the distance. She thought about their life in the small town, how everything had been so comfortable and familiar. But lately, it seemed like everything was falling apart.

Buck leaned forward, his eyes fixed on the road ahead. His jaw was set, and Sally May could see the muscles tensing in his arms.

"We can't keep running forever," she said softly.

Buck turned to look at her, his gaze softening. "I know, darlin'. But right now, we just need to get away from all this."

They drove for hours, the radio low and the wind whistling through their hair. Eventually, they found themselves in a quiet little coastal town. The ocean stretched out before them, dark and glittering under the moonlight.

"Here we are," Buck said softly.

Sally May smiled, her heart lifting as they stepped out of the car and breathed in the salty air. It was peaceful here, far away from all their problems.

As they walked along the beach, hand in hand, Sally May knew that no matter what happened next, as long as she had Buck by her side, everything would be okay.

The End.

© Aaron Abilene

Don't miss out!

Visit the website below and you can sign up to receive emails whenever Aaron Abilene publishes a new book. There's no charge and no obligation.

https://books2read.com/r/B-A-YOIP-EXGMC

BOOKS 2 READ

Connecting independent readers to independent writers.

Also by Aaron Abilene

Carnival Game
Full Moon Howl
Donovan
Shades of Z

Deadeye
Deadeye & Friends

Island
Paradise Island
The Lost Island
The Lost Island 2
The Island 2

Prototype
The Compound

Slacker
Slacker 2
Slacker: Dead Man Walkin'

Thomas
Quarantine
Contagion

Zombie Bride
Zombie Bride
Zombie Bride 2
Zombie Bride 3

Standalone
The Victims of Pinocchio
A Christmas Nightmare
Pain
Fat Jesus
A Zombie's Revenge
505
The Headhunter
Crash
Tranq
The Island
Dog
The Quiet Man

Joe Superhero
Feral
Good Guys
Devil Child of Texas
Romeo and Juliet and Zombies
The Gamer
Becoming Alpha
Dead West
Small Town Blues
Killer Claus
Alligator Allan
10 Days
Army of The Dumbest Dead
Kid
Me Again
Maurice and Me
Sparkles The Vampire Clown
She's Psycho
Vicious Cycle
Romeo and Juliet: True Love Conquers All
Random Acts of Stupidity
The Abducted

9 798223 811534